PBK

HEATHCLIFF'S TALE
by Emma Tennant

Can evil be passed from one generation to the next? Or is it born out of deprivation and despair? Does it linger, long after the death of the evil-doer—and can it haunt chillingly through the pages of a book?

Emma Tennant's new novel, *Heathcliff's Tale*, is the story of the haunting of Henry Newby, a young man despatched to Haworth Parsonage shortly after the death of Emily Brontë to retrieve a novel by Ellis Bell for his uncle, publisher of *Wuthering Heights*. He soon finds himself adrift in a sea of possibilities: are the pages which burn on the study fire the work of fiction which his uncle awaits, or, as he believes, do they comprise the confessions of a wicked man, a murderer who has brought destruction and misery to all he meets? Who *is* this Heathcliff who spills his black soul among the flames and ashes?

Heathcliff's Tale brings together a ghost story, a depiction of the marriage of Heathcliff and Isabella, and a satire on Brontë academic studies. Fact and fiction are intertwined as we are confronted with the enigma of Emily Brontë. How could a young woman with no apparent experience of passion or knowledge of evil, have summoned up Heathcliff?

. . . And Henry, as he reads on in the freezing upper chamber where he is placed for the night at Haworth Parsonage, finds himself the host of the dead Emily . . .

HEATHCLIFF'S TALE

TALE

Emma Tennant

Tartarus Press

Heathcliff's Tale
by Emma Tennant

Heathcliff's Tale is published by Tartarus Press, MMV
at Coverley House, Carlton-in-Coverdale,
Leyburn, North Yorkshire, DL8 4AY. UK.

ISBN 1872621 92 9

HEATHCLIFF'S TALE

FAMILY TREE

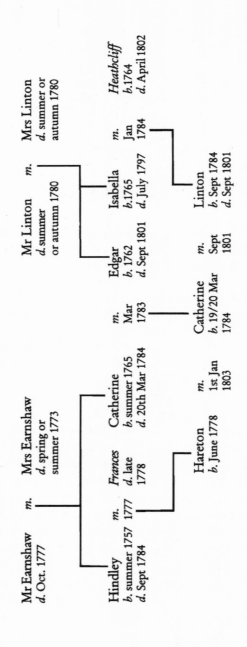

PREFACE

EDITOR'S NOTE

The following pages may help to elucidate one of literature's greatest enigmas: viz. the origins of the most evil hero ever to be portrayed. The second puzzle lies in tracing the causes and reasons behind the authorship of the great novel in which this demonic figure appears. How could a young woman with no experience of the world—or, indeed, of passion —have brought into being a man such as Heathcliff?

We are empowered in this quest for the truth behind the writing of Wuthering Heights by the appearance at auction at the saleroom in York of fragments of a novel and a cache of letters, including a 'Deposition' by a certain Henry Newby, who declares himself the nephew of Thomas Cautley Newby, publisher of Emily Brontë's now-celebrated novel. It seems the writings are genuine—although an altercation has already broken out between various factions: biographers of the Brontës and libraries amongst them. We will not go in detail into these disagreements, except to say that Branwellites and Emily-supporters are evenly distributed, when it comes to deciding the thorny problem of whose hand was responsible for this 'second novel', parts of which are presented here. Saved from the fire commanded by Charlotte Brontë in the weeks after her younger sister's death, and augmented by the strange adventures of young Master Newby as he sought the manuscript for which his unscrupulous uncle had despatched

1

him, these pages provide what is possibly the sole authentic glimpse into the early life of the orphan and evil-doer, Heathcliff.

As we are constantly reminded of the actions, the romance and the violence in Wuthering Heights, *it is pertinent here to include a brief résumé of that novel, as well as a Family Tree. The Brontës also may require some description, for those who have escaped the industry now grown up around their history. Without these, the reader might find himself as confused as poor Henry Newby.*

Briefly, Wuthering Heights *is a tale of obsession; that of Heathcliff—the lad found wandering on the streets of Liverpool by old Mr Earnshaw and taken back with him to The Heights to live with the family—for Cathy, Earnshaw's daughter; and of her obsession with him. They are separated when Cathy foolishly declares to the housekeeper, Nelly Dean, that she wishes instead to marry Edgar Linton, their well-born neighbour at Thrushcross Grange. The tragedy which then evolves, continues to the next generation, with a daughter, young Cathy, born of the Linton union but almost certainly the daughter of Heathcliff. The portions of narrative we have been fortunate enough to acquire at the York auction throw considerable light on the otherwise not depicted consummation of the passion of Heathcliff and Cathy.*

The Brontës, who famously lived at Haworth Parsonage, were originally a family of five daughters and a son, Branwell. Emily and Branwell were a year apart in age, and it was on Emily that the burden of caring for an increasingly dissolute brother fell. Her symbiotic relationship with her brother lasted to the grave: after Branwell died—in September 1848—Emily succumbed to the family disease of consumption and survived him by only three months. In this previously unknown collection of letters and documents we see the effects of that burden on the highly imaginative child; and we begin to understand the origins of Heathcliff.

HEATHCLIFF'S TALE

CHAPTER ONE

Letter from Henry Newby, Newby & Sons, Lawyers, Redhill Drive, Leeds to his uncle Thomas Cautley Newby, Publisher, 15 Mortimer Street, off Cavendish Square, London, W.1.

January 3rd 1849

Dear Uncle

I am back at home, but not without risking life and limb—and, if I may say so, a sense of my continuing sanity—while attempting to fulfil your request to retrieve a manuscript from the address you kindly supplied.

I believe I should have been given more time to fulfil this task. A solicitor's clerk, as I have no hesitation in describing my occupation (for all your urgings that my father should promote me and for all that he is your brother and should manifest pride, as you care to term it, in the achievements of his youngest son)—a solicitor's clerk, as I am and must remain, dear Uncle, cannot be expected to be a literary man. There are matters to be seen to at Newby & Sons which are daily in need of urgent attention; there is little opportunity to read books or dwell on arcane subjects; and if my brothers, the sons my respected

father has elected as Partners in the firm, can be seen
to be more advanced than I in the scaling of Parna-
ssus, I am contented to permit the situation to rest
that way. Or was, at least, until the journey into Hell
which resulted from the avuncular demand that I
should journey west of Leeds to Haworth and return with a book not yet bound and totally lacking
in description. I cannot and do not care to sound a
note of reproach, yet it occurs to me that I was ill-
chosen for this singular and distasteful errand. One
of my brothers would have done better, I hear you
agree: but it goes without saying that Horace and
Richard were both engaged in seasonal festivities
over the past week and thus were unable to obey
your command.

So it was I, Henry, who was obliged to see in
the New Year at Haworth Parsonage, a circumstance
so chilling it should not be recounted here. I own,
to my considerable distress, that the suffering I endured cannot be committed to paper, for I lack the
ability to do so. If you had despatched a literary man,
Uncle, I do not doubt the resulting account would
swell the coffers at 15 Mortimer Street.

The journey, undertaken on the gloomiest night
of the year—the last, and seeing itself out with a
wild storm, this punctuated by a north-east wind
such as we never experience in Redhill Drive, pro-
tected as that thoroughfare is by its low-lying position in the central part of the city—was no more
than a faint foretaste of what was to come. I thought
myself unfortunate to be set down by the coach at
the foot of a steep hill which constitutes Haworth's
main street, for I was rapidly soaked to the skin by
flurries of rain blown along what was no more than
a cobbled tunnel by the rising wind. I considered
myself ill-favoured once more when a local, barely

comprehensible in his dialect, misdirected me right out of the town and up to the gates of a house that had, as I was informed by an angry caretaker, no connection with the church. But even then I had no inkling of the evil fate which awaited me, when eventually I found the address written out so clearly, dear Uncle, in your letter. I could not have known, for all its forbidding exterior and despite the grim landscape of moor and bog that stretch behind the house, that I was about to experience a sensation akin to the abandoning of hope.

But this is not the account you attend with such impatience, Uncle. Your letter warned me that I would find a grieving household: the author of the manuscript I was to fetch had recently died and the family, having suffered another death only a few months before, might make difficulties at first when I came with my demand. I was to persevere, if this was the case—for, as Thomas Cautley Newby, publisher, of London, you had paid an advance of £25 to the lately deceased author (if works by his predecessor to the grave were offered to me I was not to take them) and the manuscript is the property of Thomas Cautley Newby. Our family firm of Newby & Sons confirmed the legality of this before I set out; though, given the above information, I felt less and less willing to obey instructions. The oddity of the late author's identity was also a factor in my growing reluctance to undertake this commission for you, Uncle: I must confess I thought you must be confused when you directed me to search for the papers of one writer, but that I would be admitted by another who would prove to be a brother or sister of the author. You would not state more, and could have saved me great discomfort and unease if you had done so. But, as you remark clearly enough

in your missive, it is not possible to know yet whether the manuscript, once found, is to be published
pseudonymously or not. With these anxieties pressing closely on me, I found myself at last outside the
door of Haworth Parsonage. I had already attempted, by stopping at the sexton's cottage, to learn
more of the household I was about to enter, but my
luck being as already described, there came no answer to my repeated knocking. So it became clear
there was no alternative but to address myself to the
front door of the Parsonage, and I did so, but in
great trepidation. It was pitch dark, I may add, Uncle,
and your favourite nephew, as you were pleased in
the past to address me, was as cold and wet as a dog
that has fallen in the beck, swollen now in the cut
of dead grass on the moor.

The door was opened after what seemed an age
and a face peered up at me. I must have been forced
forward by a strong gust of the nor-easterly, for I
found myself almost falling on an elderly little woman, at least sixty years old I should say, and as dis-
comfited as I was by my appearance, unattended, in
the front hall of the Parsonage.

'Mister Newby' said the old lady (I had of course
written 'To Whom It May Concern' to introduce my
coming arrival, but had received no reply). 'Mister
Newby, Miss Charlotte does not expect you here,
sir. She wrote—did the letter not arrive at—at—'

'In Leeds', I said with more irritation than I had
intended to express. 'My uncle, Thomas Newby, asks
me to collect a manuscript from the Parsonage at
Haworth. A manuscript', I added, for my legal training did not desert me now it was needed, 'which is
the property of the publishing firm of Thomas Cautley Newby, Mortimer Street, London'.

If it did not occur to me to wonder who this guardian of the mysterious manuscript could be—for the old harridan barred the door leading from the hall to what I assumed to be the kitchen, with arms as lined and frail as the branches of a dying sapling—this was because a smaller door in a corner of the hall had swung open in the draught made by my entrance and I was able to see into a room, book-lined, comfortably provided with a fire and, so far as I could see at least, empty.

'Your Miss—Miss Charlotte', I said, 'will I find her at home tonight? She will perhaps deliver the book to me?'

'Tabby!' came a peremptory voice, a woman's, from somewhere else again. 'You have been instructed to show Mr Newby to the door if he should come here searching for Ellis Bell'.

'Yes, Miss Charlotte', said old Tabby, but in a quiet tone which must have been inaudible anywhere else than the exiguous vestibule where we stood, she still preventing me from entering and I as obdurate as ever. But Tabby had seen the extent of the weathering I had taken, I suppose, and she must have observed, too, my frantic glances at the comfortable little room where an oil-lamp lit up a pleasant sequence of water-colour sketches of the Lakes that hung on the walls and a good old clock stood in the corner, its second hand ticking as if to announce a permanent haven could be found here. Her arms fell to her sides and she looked at me uncertainly.

'He has been shown the door, this odious Mr Newby, has he not?' came the female voice, more strident now and, so it seemed to me, emanating from the upper floor of the simple dwelling. 'Lock the door behind him, Tabby, for the love of God!

And come to help me—fetch the next bundle of
papers—'

With a shove in the small of my back quite sur-
prising from one so ill-endowed as this old housekeeper, I found myself propelled into the sitting-
room. The door that shut behind me was an inner
door, not the forbidding oak which would have
closed against me if Tabby had obeyed her orders,
yet this door, as I immediately ascertained, boasted
a key of its own; and this I turned in the lock, much
to the discomfiture of the old woman outside. 'Mr
Newby—don't fasten the door, sir—Miss Charlotte
will be down directly. Warm yourself at the fire, Mr
Newby, but unlock the door, I beg you!'

Tabby's cries, dear Uncle, were in vain. I may
not have succeeded in my father's eyes, finding the
law examinations most unworthy and unfair in their
expectations, but I flatter myself that I am quick to
grasp an opportunity when one arises. This opportunity, you must undoubtedly agree, saved a situation here which I have no doubt will prove of the
greatest import to you. For, while expressing my
grateful awareness that no kinsman of a Newby
would relish their relative falling ill after a good
soaking, I am also cognisant of the fact that there
are hopes of a large sum of money to be made from
this sought manuscript—though why and what it
contains I knew nothing of whatsoever on my arrival
at the Parsonage.

In the event, I wasted no time in surveying the
cheerful room, taking care to warm myself as best I
might as I did so. The chairs, I noted, were unlikely
to conceal manuscripts or hidden papers, as their
springs seemed broken, and the cretonne covers in
which they had long been clad were too threadbare
to hold a burgeoning bundle of any kind. A dog-

basket, promising at first with its rumpled cushion
and wickerwork surround, turned out to contain
only a bone or two and a knitted garment, much
chewed and spat on. As the room was now silent,
Tabby having I suppose gone upstairs to confer
with her mistress on the subject of the stranger
locked in the sitting-room, I took advantage of the
blaze from the lighted coals in the grate and knelt
on the hearth a moment. And it was here, under a
rug fashioned from rags and scraps of material, that
I saw a hump, which I took at first for a bag of
further ingredients for such rag rugs as ladies of
uncertain means are taught to make. The bag,
when pulled out onto the boards, turned out to be
stuffed not with cotton or chintz, but with paper—
with pages, in fact—and you will forgive me, dear
Uncle, if I say that a shout of triumph, smothered,
naturally, was succeeded by a groan on my observing that further pages smouldered just a few inches
from my face, that is in the fire.

I am not known for courage in times such as
this—but for the sake of the eminent publishing
firm of Thomas Cautley Newby I acted with a daring
and precision as astonishing to myself, dear Uncle,
as it would have been to you. I stretched out my
arm, picked up the tongs, and, despite the dreadful
proximity of the hot coals, extracted the pages that
flickered merrily there.

At this moment, the handle of the sitting-room
door turned several times, impatiently, and a voice,
a man's voice, gruff and irritable in the extreme,
called out 'Tabby! Is that you, Tabby, in there? Miss
Charlotte shall have more tea, as she asks, I pre-
sume? And the potatoes are overdone again—Tabby,
where the devil are you?'

The strangest fact to report here is the total silence and peace which descended on the Parsonage shortly after this outburst. I heard a woman, either Tabby or the 'Miss Charlotte' from upstairs, come along the hall, and the door, which must have been the door to the kitchen, close behind her just as she spoke in a comforting tone to the man. I awaited the furious arrival of Tabby or Miss Charlotte. But no one came; the clock ticked; a dog scratched at the door once and then, snuffling, went away.

I cannot give an idea of the time I spent in solitary seclusion in the sitting-room at Haworth on that New Year's Eve. I am told that literary pursuits —reading, in short—can alter time and provide an illusion of hours or seconds passing, depending on the tale which proceeds to unfurl.

I had only the charred and singed pages just rescued from the well-blacked and polished grate, in my two hands. The bag with other fragments lay at my feet. And when I was at last disturbed I had not consumed as much as that domestic blaze had been about to do. But I cannot vouchsafe, dear Uncle, so rapt was my attention, the length of time I passed in the landscape described in those pages, in the sitting-room of Haworth Parsonage that night. I was plunged half-a-century back, and I read the account of Mr Lockwood on his visit to these parts as if he wrote solely for your loyal nephew, Henry Newby.

CHAPTER TWO

JOSEPH LOCKWOOD'S RETURN

1802—I am just back from a visit to my former landlord at Wuthering Heights, Mr Heathcliff, and I am sorely distressed at the change in him since my visit in the autumn of last year. In September I saw a vigorous man, older and wiser perhaps than I had known him in those days of which Mrs Dean, the excellent housekeeper, tells to such chilling effect. Now, there would be no question of my lodging at The Heights, as I had hoped to do: my landlord is weak and unable to bear the presence of a stranger for more than an hour at a time. 'You will find accommodation at Thrushcross Grange, Mr Lockwood', Mr Heathcliff informed me, and even in his deteriorated condition it was possible to detect a scornful glint in his eye as he spoke. 'Nelly Dean is there. She will put you up and feed you with some amusing tales, I do not doubt, not least the account of the deaths of so many you must have felt you knew as your own family, Mr Lockwood, so garrulously did our housekeeper regale you with their exploits.'

I hung my head, not wishing to admit that an insatiable curiosity had indeed drawn me north once more to the bleak moorland and deep valleys of The Heights and Gimmerton Vale. Before I could look up, however, it was clear that the sick man, propping himself further on his pillows, had decided to entertain me as Nelly Dean had once done: he had a tale to tell, and—uncharitable though my conclusions may have been—I could not refrain from reflecting that Mr Heathcliff had in all probability decided to make a last testament, finding it easier to confide in an outsider than to anyone closer to the wicked life he had led.

'I saw young Miss Cathy', I put in, 'and I was glad to note she was in excellent health. When I last found myself in these parts, she had the kindness to invite me to her marriage with—with your son—'

'Linton is dead', said Heathcliff. As I could not help from noticing, colour crept into his cheeks as he spoke, and a sparkle in his eye suggested all was not yet finished with him. An awful thought even came to me that this man, considered mad, or a devil (for all that he owns The Heights and much of the surrounding countryside) might leap from his bed and take his fist to me if I had the folly of speaking in his presence. Accordingly I fell silent; and after a brief pause, my landlord—as I was to discover, Heathcliff was now also proprietor of Thrushcross Grange—continued with his speech.

'Yes, Linton was as lily-livered—as feeble-minded also—as the family whose name he bore. Linton Heathcliff, indeed! The knave was all Linton, his mother to the core, a whining, complaining ninny pampered by the wretched Isabella with no thought for his coming manhood: a girl in breeches, a pompous, pretentious fool!'

'But when did he die?' I dared to ask, for Heathcliff seemed now to have sunk into a black mood recognisable from my past visits to The Heights. 'Miss Cathy—I mean to say, Mrs Heathcliff—must have been distressed in the extreme by so terrible a happening shortly after her marriage—'

'Don't count on it!' Heathcliff replied with a chuckle. He reached for a cigar, lying on the table next to his bed, and lit it, this followed by much coughing and spluttering. 'She's training up young Hareton, son of the late and unlamented Hindley Earnshaw, to be her next suitor. He has to learn to read first, before he can sign any marriage lines with the widow Catherine Heathcliff. But he makes progress, I am happy to announce'.

I decided to say as little as possible in reply to this. Heathcliff's motive for informing me of the coming marriage of young Cathy would doubtless be revealed and soon, for, as I remembered, no one liked to boast more than this man. He had come from nowhere, and no one knew so much as his name when old Joseph Earnshaw rescued a lost and abandoned child in the streets of Liverpool some thirty-seven years ago. Regarded by Edgar Linton, the gentle-natured squire of The Grange as little more than a ploughboy or stable lad—and with a touch of the Lascar, as Nelly's employer Mr Linton had sometimes liked to add—Heathcliff had now made a considerable fortune. His mortgaging of The Heights to old Joseph Earnshaw's son Hindley, had been little short of a stroke of genius, for the drunken gambler soon lost all he possessed to his former servant and foster-brother. That Heathcliff encouraged the union of Hindley's son to young Cathy, must promise something beneficial to Heathcliff, ill and resigned to his coming end though he might be.

'So your daughter-in-law Cathy—' I said, and stopped on seeing a look that was more pain and anger cross his features. He could be handsome still, I saw, when the sun came in on his dark eyes and features—and I wondered, for a mad moment, whether he suffered from a passion for his daughter-in-law Cathy, daughter of the love of his life, the long-dead Catherine Earnshaw.

'If you wonder why young Cathy stays here with me at The Heights following the death of the milksop who was her husband, then I must inform you that there is a good reason why she is here, even though she still considers The Grange to be her home: indeed, she prays often to return there'.

'But—'

'Edgar Linton, Cathy's father is also dead', Heathcliff said. He smiled fully into my face as he spoke and the cigar, now extinguished for lack of interest by its owner, rolled from the battered table top onto the floor. 'Can you imagine that I mourn him, Mr Lockwood? No, I do not—and I daresay it was due to my own actions that Mr Linton died. When he lay ill in bed and The Grange had neither Nelly nor footmen indoors or out—I took advantage of the opportunity to hasten poor Mr Edgar's departure from this world'.

'What do you mean?' I in turn could not resist interrupting him. Heathcliff, now leaning into the room and therefore approaching me too near for my own inclination, had, I saw, altered his smile to something more like a grin. I began to wish myself miles away, beyond Gimmerton and out in the freshness of a landscape which did not contain my host or any member of the Linton or Earnshaw tribes. I wondered, indeed, if I had been right to break off my tranquil visit to the Lakes with this incursion into a demonic mind.

'I told Mr Edgar Linton', Heathcliff said, and having seen me glance round the room like one trapped by fire or some other natural disaster, he went so far as to grab hold of my wrist and hold it down tight on the table top. 'I told the man whom my love, my life, my unforgettable and dead darling, Cathy, had in her youthful folly married in my absence—and I revenged myself, too late —alas! too late—I told the weak-kneed idiot Edgar that I had visited his house many times on my return from America—'

'Yes, Mr Heathcliff', I said, and tried as politely as possible to remove my hand from the prison of his hot grasp. 'I believe Nelly told anyone who wished to hear that her employer Mrs Linton, Cathy, had shown great pleasure and excitement when you announced yourself at The Grange and paid a call on Mrs Linton and her husband. You reminded Mr Edgar of this as he lay ill in bed, perhaps?' I added, privately thinking that if this was the case it had been a cruel thing to do. Heathcliff sprang to his feet. He seemed to have restored his spirits since beginning to talk of Cathy, HIS Cathy, as it were, and I no longer saw him as a failing man.

'No, you dolt', came the reply, in a voice that was quiet, angry and amused at the same time. 'I informed my dead Cathy's husband that I had taken possession of his wife, that I had made love to the woman who had been mine, body and soul, since we were children. This had been the purpose of my visits to The Grange. Now what do you think of that, Mr Lockwood?'

☙

The manuscript continued with the single word 'Heathcliff'. Below is his account—so I took it to be his dismissal by his childhood sweetheart Cathy, and his flight from home, followed by the adventures related to Mr Lockwood.

☙

'I heard the words at the door and I ran. It was a dark night and the moor had opened up in treacherous bogs and ponds, impossible to see or avoid. It had closed hard against me too, with outcrops of rock sharp as knives now the recent rains had flattened their mossy covering.

'I ran, at first without direction, tracking like an animal in what I gauged was the way to Peniston Crag. But I knew I ran in circles, when the mountain, revealing itself to me through gaps in the racing black cloud, loomed high above me twice. I was lost, and I had lost more than my knowledge of the moor at The Heights, that night. I feared—I knew only fear, as I remember: all other emotion had gone—I feared more than the prospect of my own death in one of those bottomless pits of black water, that my feet would lead me back to the house I had just left forever. The house where I had been brought as a child; where I had learned to speak and then to love. I could not go back there, yet my feet seemed to pull me towards a glimmer of light, no more than a marsh-glow, as I knew, a glimmer which could be the lantern at the door where Nelly stood over the stove, looking out for me from the kitchen.

'The tree at the Gimmerton crossroads came at me like a friend and an enemy together. Here, we had kissed, Cathy and I—here, still, on nights when the moon relented and left its cloudy caverns to shine on those who walked the rough road to Gimmerton, she and I met again and I clasped a ghost while crying aloud in my desire to join her in the grave. Then the wind would blow across the moor and she would vanish in my arms, no more than a wraith, a figment of my fevered imagination. Here, men had been hung, and had died, for the tree was as much a gallows as a trysting-place. And here, as I ran from the fresh attack of freezing rain that came now from the west, was my refuge, at last. I knew where I was; and I knew where I had to go.

'I will not give in detail the horrors and griefs of my arduous journey. The horror lay in the almost physical sickness which afflicted me as I walked the long road to the city, this alleviated at the last by a kindly waggon-driver, who set me down on the outskirts of Liverpool.

From there, as if I could already smell the sea and savour the bitterness of my escape from the only world I had ever known, I went to the docks. A rat could not have gone with surer instinct to a shipload of cane sugar than I to the harbour; a serpent could not have wound itself more cunningly than I did that night in the hold of an unsuspecting ship destined for distant shores.

'I did not rest until I knew myself secure amongst the cases and barrels bound for the New World—for CAROLINA was stamped everywhere—and I heard from the shouts and conversations above my head that at dawn we would sail to America. Once the hold was fastened down I made myself comfortable on a sack of flour and I began to feel excitement at my impending departure to a world where a war raged, as I knew from the talk of the gentry brought over from The Grange, and there were many dead and wounded. I knew myself to be on the side of those who fought the British. The enemy I saw as smiling, fair and sweet-mannered as the odious Edgar Linton.

'I had bread and water and a flagon of spirits, seized from a tavern where the girl who believed I had love or at least lust in my heart for her, went willingly to the kitchens to procure them. But I felt nothing, neither love nor hatred nor gratitude, to anyone. By the time my little servant had handed me the food, she had seen my eyes and already shrank from me. She saw, I have no doubt, the wound inflicted on me that night: the dark moor, the lovely face of Cathy framed by the larder door outside, the stable where I had been taught to belong by her cursed brother Hindley. And my little helper must have heard, too, the words which sounded so loud and repeated again and again in my ears, the words with which my one and only love informed Nelly Dean that she would marry Edgar Linton.

'The journey was as long as time and as short as a passing dream. I saw the dawn and darkness through a crack in the roof of the hold. I took the ship's biscuits and rum and water the half-witted cabin boy, finding me there one night when ordered to dig for provisions in a barrel, brought me in exchange for the card games and tricks I taught him. For a Gypsy, as Master Hindley Earnshaw would be pleased to say, does not travel without his Tarot or his faking cards. I told the lad a hundred times over that he was born under the sign of the Sun and would find fortune in the far-off lands where we would one day drop anchor. But I felt no belief in this: the chap was a blackamoor and dwarfish to boot, and I expected the Captain to abandon him on some marshy island when once we came to our destination.

'Of all the good fortune that ever smiled on this poor creature you see before you—a broken man, you might say, Mr Lockwood, even if ownership of both The Heights and Thrushcross Grange may bestow some distinction in the neighbourhood, I am not deluded as to the obloquy which attends my every action—the most outstanding was that of discovering myself, once we were arrived in Carolina, to be in the middle of a most well-placed battle. Well-placed, because it took me not more than an hour to pull off the redcoat of a dying soldier on the ground and assume a different identity.

'But I go too fast for you, sir. You must understand, as of course I did at a later date, that the battle of Eutaw Creek was the last in the American war; that the chaos and confusion which reigned there made dissimulation easy and daughters of prosperous landowners as desperate to catch a handsome soldier as their fathers were agreeable to the prospect. Many were ruined, others were in a state of panic that the holdings they had built up in the Colony would be lost in the war. And I, poor Heathcliff, stable lad at Wuthering Heights, orphan and dis-

carded brother of Catherine Earnshaw and her drunken
devil of a true brother, Hindley, lost no time in taking on
the swagger of the blood-stained uniform I had seized,
and of hinting at a substantial fortune left behind in the
old country.

'You may frown at me, for taking a woman without
any love for her and of promising to cherish the wretch
for all her days. But I did just this. I needed the gold which
would one day bring me back to Cathy. For I knew she
could not mean what she had vowed to Nelly, that she
would marry the feeble-hearted Linton and bear him
children in the gentry world of which neither she nor I
could ever be a part. I knew she lied—even if she thought
me nowhere near and had no notion that I heard her
silly prattle—she lied to herself and to the foolish old
housekeeper too, to keep up her spirits in our hopeless
situation.

'Do not imagine I hadn't tried a thousand times to
find a way of extricating us from the prison of my poverty
and the impossibility of our union. There was never an
answer to my prayers—whether I addressed Satan or the
Lord Jesus Christ who is shown to us as possessing the
mild manners of a Linton. Nothing and nobody supplied
the answer. I would live and die amongst the animals,
where old Earnshaw's heir had so happily imprisoned
me.

'But here, in the New World, a gallant captain, all
fortune smiled on me.

'And so I married Louisa—as her name was—but
already, I must confess, I forget her face.

'Things settled down and I became a farmer. My
father-in-law, glad to get his daughter off his hands,
increased the acreage when I told him of the moors and

fields and grazing lands I owned here. For I informed the old fool that if there was any ever trouble in Carolina, he and his wife could accompany us to England, to my estates.

'Yet I could feel no satisfaction with my new prosperity, for I dreamed day and night of Cathy. I wanted no one else, and the hours passed with my new wife became a game to me, where I would half-close my eyes and see my darling there instead—in the hammock on the verandah of our lovely house, or across from me at the mahogany table piled with luscious fruits and fine glazed meats and hams. I saw my Cathy there, wife and hostess—but soon in my fevered thoughts we'd run away together and go into the marshes, as muddy and dangerous as the moor where we belonged. We'd kiss and fall there amongst the spiky grasses.

'I don't know if Louisa guessed any of this, but it soon became clear to me that my restlessness could be cured only by travelling and by gaining a real fortune— enough, in short, to transport me back to Yorkshire a rich and respected man.

'I told my wife—I recall it was a poignant scene— that I must leave her for six months and make my way to Jamaica. We all knew I meant to build up a fortune on plantations bought with my wife's money, but nothing was said on the subject.

'The mistake made by my faithful spouse was, I suppose, inevitable. She announced she would come with me, and could not be persuaded otherwise. Whether she saw in me the evil intentions which immediately filled my mind, I cannot say. It was true that her mother had long suspected me—but of being a member of a dark race, not of the murderous plan which now occupied me day and night.

'We embarked on a slave-ship to Jamaica four weeks later. I would prefer, Mr Lockwood, to leave subsequent events unspoken, but this is impossible—for I have not long to live and my story must be fully told. I returned from Jamaica to Liverpool a very rich man, Mr Lockwood. We shall go downstairs now and take a glass of wine, before I resume.'

CHAPTER THREE

Letter from Henry Newby to Thomas Cautley Newby.

January 4th 1849

Dear Uncle,

You must forgive the pause—of very short duration, I sincerely hope—which follows on from my
last, abruptly terminated missive to you. When once
the circumstances are understood, I know you will
forgive your dutiful and loving nephew. There are,
as you are sure to concur, times when politenesses
and formalities, generally observed in the writing
and addressing of letters and the like, cannot be observed. One of these must be the accounting of my
own grim experience in the study at Haworth Parsonage on New Year's Eve last, when to read the confessions of a murderer and to find oneself alone with
what must have been a ghost, contributed, as I know
you will comprehend, to a state of mind far removed from that of a composed gentleman.

In short, Uncle, I do wish most earnestly that it
was not I who had been despatched on this errand.
Literary gifts—or rather, the lack of them—no longer seem to be of import here: rather, the apprehen-
sion and arrest of a criminal, not the appreciating of
a work of art, is in question. For I have no doubt
whatsoever that the monstrous author of the pages I

rescued from the fire is a killer, and that he will kill again.

The task of copying to you the dreadful confession on charred and singed paper which I have recounted to you, is too disagreeable, not to say terrifying, for me to be able to do so.

I shall therefore supply you—and as a publisher I have little doubt that you will find a writer both easily and cheaply to make this a story with potential for good sales—with the final details of the incriminating pages I took—and now deeply regret having done so—from the fire at the house to which you directed me.

It is possible that you may be able to trace Mr Lockwood to whom the brute gave his account? Our firm will do all to assist you. The unprincipled thief, impostor and—almost certain—wife-killer of whom you have been reading is named Heathcliff. This braggart in a dead Captain's uniform took some time before being able or willing to own up to his true appellation; it was immediately clear there had been no baptism of the little stray picked up in the streets of Liverpool by a kindly landowner, a Mr Joseph Earnshaw; and that the bastard, dark-skinned as a Lascar, had been encouraged to regard his position in the family as a blood member, a mistake sometimes encountered at Newby & Sons, when a Will is contested by a person once adopted and then discarded by a distinguished family.

As my father, dear Uncle, has often remarked, this illusion of equal prospects when entertained by an outsider, can lead only to trouble. And in the case of Heathcliff—named after a son of the Earnshaws who had apparently died in infancy—the trouble was not cauterised, as it should have been, by the expulsion of the child when once his ungodly and vituperative nature was clear. Heathcliff was permitted to remain at The Heights—as he refers to it: do you know, Uncle, of any information as to the whereabouts of this place? My father had not heard the name, though my brother Horace remarked that he'd heard recently of a farmhouse, very isolated, that had a similar title: Top Withins.

However that may be, Master Hindley Earnshaw, once the old man had died, soon put the unChristian creature in his place, where he was to remain as stable lad. There was even—and now, with both parents dead there was only an elderly housekeeper, Nelly Dean, to say yea or nay to friendships and associations formed by the children in this lonely spot—a passion, if one is to believe the pages drawn from a blaze where they should, once consigned to the flames, have remained. The passion between Heathcliff and Hindley Earnshaw's sister Cathy is referred to endlessly. I was both sickened and ashamed to read of it; and, not for the first time, complimented in my mind the person who had decided to dispose of the confession—Tabby, the maid who had admitted me earlier, so I came to think.

There is worse to come, Uncle, than an admission of a totally unsuitable infatuation for the late landowner's daughter. Had this been the most heinous crime owned to in the pages, I could in all probability have set the bundle of paper down and gone in search of the true cause of my visit to Haworth Parsonage, i.e. the retrieval of a late author's manuscript. But there was something so horrifying—so inhuman, one might say, in what I read, that I did not feel it any other than a moral obligation to continue reading—and this, as you know me since my early years, has not been an occupation to find favour in my eyes. I confess here also that I no longer considered myself confronted with the fantasies of a fecund brain; rather the finder of a true rendition of evil.

For your sake—and for mine, too, I shall summarise.

The ship with Heathcliff and his wife as sole passengers on the journey out, sailed to Jamaica and returned to Bristol fully laden with cotton and sugar.

Mr and Mrs Heathcliff (I refuse the false title of Captain for the scoundrel) were not on board on the return journey. We are informed—this in a page which the devout Tabby had pushed right to the rear of the grate so nearly half was burnt and thus illegible—that Heathcliff, wooing his wife with false promises, then hired a sloop and proceeded to make a tour of the Grenadine and Windward islands, stopping the longest time in the south of St Lucia, where a family of friendly natives welcomed the visitors from the New World.

Here, in a stretch of land dedicated to the religious rites of the natives—a bay lying between the great Pitons was the site of ceremonies too appalling to recount to you here, Uncle—Heathcliff 'lost' his wife Louisa. I cannot say whether his account suggests sacrifice, cannibalism or any other heathen practice: what appears to be the case is that little or no effort was made to save poor Louisa from her fate.

Heathcliff, it pains me to relate, shows neither grief nor compunction at his spouse's death. He returns to Carolina, comforts with all his usual vile hypocrisy the devastated parents of Louisa; and then departs for England with her fortune in his hands.

Most distressing of all, Uncle, is the fact that one name, one woman, haunts Mr Heathcliff as he

26

makes his way back to the city which saw the evil day of his birth, namely Liverpool.

The name is Cathy. He believes he will return to marry her, with his new wealth. Cathy, Cathy . . . you must forgive me, Uncle, if I say the sense of this passion quite overcame me as I read.

As I laid down the last page, the handle of the study door was turned and I leapt to my feet, abashed I must confess, at the turmoil of emotions occasioned by reading the confessions of this wicked man. Amongst these troubling sensations lay the suspicion that someone in this very house must be the author of these awful crimes, and so must be responsible for the charred pages. These I stuffed into my satchel, taking care to push in also the bag under the rag rug, and as I reached the door to turn the key, found a knife had slipped the lock, causing the door to swing open in my face.

A tall man stood facing me. You will forgive me, Uncle, when I say I thought the features, strong and brooding as they were, could be those of the villain, Heathcliff. You must pardon my heightened state of excitement, and thus my lack of judgement in this matter.

'Mr Heathcliff?' I said, noting my voice was as tremulous as a girl's.

Uncle, you know the rest. A man of God stood before me. He looked sternly down at me and asked why I had been 'left in here': what did Charlotte think she was doing, to forget me?

My host—as he turned out to be—then introduced himself as the Reverend Patrick Brontë.

January 24th 1849

Dear Uncle,

You must forgive me yet again, Uncle, for delaying in despatching to you this latest instalment of my account of the visit, suggested by yourself, to Haworth Parsonage on New Year's Eve. The mission to 'rescue', as you termed it, a manuscript by a late author, Mr Ellis Bell, has been a trying, not to say, disagreeable one, puzzling as well as actually terrifying in its mish-mash of changed identities and even—though I do not expect to be believed or respected for my assertion—giving proof, if such were needed, of the existence of a world beyond ours, a world, as one might describe it, 'beyond the veil'. This aspect of my visit was the reason, I must confess, for my postponement of the posting of this last part of my letter to you: I snipped it off from the rest, I am ashamed to own, and concealed it in the drawer of the dresser in the dining-room of our house in Leeds, once I found the strength and capacity to return there. You will think me childish in my concealment of the rendition of the horrible events which befell me: you will consider your youngest nephew an unsuitable emissary, and you will doubtless transfer similar requests for the finding and rendering to you of manuscripts legally yours to my brothers Horace and Edward. I cannot feel reproach or, I must admit, sorrow, if you do. For never again will I go in search of property written by a non-existent author who, when investigated, transpires to be a ghost.

Only my determination not to betray your trust in me, dear Uncle, led me finally to open the drawer of the dresser—and, watched with some alarm by our good Susan, remove the offending last segment of the letter, seal and post it off to you. Make of it what you will. I can have no more to do with Bells, Brontës or any other person with connection past or present to Haworth Parsonage.

The Reverend Patrick Brontë, once I had come to understand that this was not the evil Mr Heathcliff whose confessions I had just read, answered my questions at first with politeness and consideration, No, Mr Ellis Bell was not at home—and nor, as the holy man continued in what I heard as a sepulchral tone, would he ever be.

'Mr Bell is—deceased, Sir?' I said, for you, Uncle, had after all informed me that the works of this late author were in your copyright for many years to come. I wished, I may assure you, solely to speed up the proceedings; and by showing I was cognisant of the sad state of Mr Bell, to assist the Reverend Mr Brontë with his search for the missing manuscript.

'Ellis Bell is not known to me', came the reply, and I could see the vicar was accustomed to chide his parishioners regularly, should they overstep the limits of good behaviour. 'You are in the wrong house, Mr Newby, and I will be grateful to find you have departed from it within the next minute.'

'But—' I began.

'Mr Newby, I believe you must have entered the Parsonage by the front door', was all I received by way of cure for my bewilderment. For if the author was not even known here, then you, Uncle, had surely been gravely mistaken in your directions. 'Ellis Bell, care of Brontë', I said, remembering your strict instruction that I should not permit myself to be 'fobbed off' by anyone attempting to hold on to the manuscript and by so doing contravene the regulations regarding copyright. Your £25, Uncle, was uppermost in my mind at that moment; and for the first time in my life I own I felt a slight stirring of interest in the law. Did I have the right, if this vicar held back the goods from me consistently, to arrest the man as a citizen and take him to the courts so that my complaint could be heard?

'You will kindly leave now, Mr Newby, or I shall call the dog', my host proceeded to announce. 'Keeper!' he shouted out, not waiting any time to carry out his threat. 'Keeper, come here!'

All I shall report from this moment on, Uncle, may seem so improbable and extraordinary as to lack veracity—but I do not lie; neither, God forbid! do I jest.

A huge dog, violent in appearance and growling menacingly, rushed from the kitchen, the door of which seemed to have been flung open by an invisible hand before closing again abruptly. At the same time, as the dog ran to sink its teeth in my leg—and it did, dear Uncle—your brother's Benjamin was grateful indeed to have secreted the bag of papers in a pocket of the greatcoat borrowed from my father, and thus doubly important as a means of evading the jaws of this Cerberus—at the same time, as I was about to confide to you, the good Lord himself intervened, though whether the Reverend Mr Brontë welcomed the intervention cannot be known.

A thunderclap—a series of thunderclaps, rather, each louder than the last—sounded right over the roof of the Parsonage. We were in darkness now, Mr Brontë and I, as he led me from the doorway of the study into the hall, and lightning in shafts of a terrible brightness pierced the pitch blackness. 'My eyes are bad', the holy man cried. 'Help me, Mr Newby, I cannot see my way to the front door!'

As might have been expected, a dreadful wind now rose, and the study door slammed shut as the strong, freezing air blew in under the portals and filled the hall with a tomb-like atmosphere. I truly thought I would die then, Uncle, and feel no shame in confessing that I was as eager to discover the front door as was Mr Brontë. I wished only to depart then, as you may imagine, and if I lacked a manuscript, I could not place this as the chief of my priorities.

But then, Uncle, as is so often the case with a thunderstorm, there came the rain. It was not ordinary rain—God save my soul, it was black rain and I could swear on that—though naturally, as it was dark outside as well as in, and I saw this through the one window of the hall, I could have been mistaken. But it was loud rain; it battered down as if a ton of hailstones had been added to the load. And when, groping along a wall, I found the door, the wind and rain together blew it shut with force right on my fingers. 'Damn you, open it!' was all the compassion I received from the gaunt old vicar at this; and I confess I thought for a moment that I led Mr Heathcliff and no other across the stone floor of the Parsonage.

When I was saved, it was by the very creature who had assisted my entrance earlier. Tabby, as I recognised she must be, pushed the kitchen door ajar and appeared, an oil-lamp in her hand. The wick was low and the flame guttered wildly; but it survived a crossing of the hall, and at her command the dog Keeper, annoyed no doubt to find a dry mouthful of cretonne and cottons for his pains, let go of me and slunk back to the kitchen. 'The gentleman cannot go out in this weather', said the crone, speaking up into the face of the parson—and very wild he looked by now, as if the storm had frightened him more even than it had me—'he can go to the upstairs study for the night, surely, Mr Brontë? There's no fire laid there—but it is best that he goes in there, as Miss Charlotte has given her consent, sir'.

So it was, Uncle, that I avoided a death by lightning or immolation on New Year's Eve at Haworth.

Yet I give my solemn word that I would give my all to have run out in the storm, however vile the consequences. For, by staying the night at the Parsonage—well, I can say merely that I might have thought myself ill-treated earlier by my hosts (and worse treated by the cruel storm that raged out across the moor)—but there was worse to come.

CHAPTER FOUR

Letter from Thomas Cautley Newby to his nephew Henry Newby.

February 3rd 1849

Dear Henry,

I am in receipt of your various missives concerning your (supremely unsuccessful) visit to Haworth Parsonage.

I will not say here that I feel shame at owning a kinsman of your intellectual calibre, which is limited indeed; for on your mother's side, as was accepted at the time of the marriage of your parents, there were—and remain still—relatives of a markedly low ability, being in some cases virtually illiterate, and certainly, in the case of Hugh who came for a week to work here as a clerk, either innumerate or frankly dishonest.

No, I will not admit to shame. But I must sound a note of reproach. Your last letter, ending as it did with the (highly improbable, indeed impossible) visitation you describe, I have destroyed, in fear that one day a descendant in this illustrious business might discover it in our files. We may deal in fiction, Master Henry—but we do not trade in lies. I can conclude only that a natural exuberance of spirits combined with strong liquor on the occasion of New

33

Year's Eve last, led you to hallucinate. What aggravates me particularly is your insistence of setting these wild flights of fantasy—a delirium, even—down on paper. Even if the account you produced had in fact been intended as fiction, no reader would have suspended their disbelief in your crazy tale. If you wish to concoct a story, dear nephew, may I suggest you open a volume—by Sir Walter Scott or another—and learn your craft. Leading a reader to believe what you put down is altogether a more difficult business than you give credence for.

So please understand that I can go as far as the door of the 'upstairs study' you describe, with you; and no further.

You state that you found the bleak small room to which the housekeeper conducted you most unwelcoming (this I can believe if the room was, as I imagine it to have been, the bedchamber of the late author whose manuscript you have not rendered to me).

You go on to remark that 'as soon as the door was closed, the terrible cold tomb-wind entered through the window; the lamp blew out; and what appeared to be a hand knocked at the lattice'.

How can this be, dear Henry? On a freezing night, a hand at the window of an upper floor? Your contention that there were repeated attempts by this 'hand' to open the lattice leaves me completely unconvinced. The bare bough of a tree, my boy, no more. And the fact you 'nearly died of fear' appears little other than the ridiculous exaggeration of a drunkard. I shall not write to your father directly on the subject of your visit to Haworth, but I shall consider doing so if this ineffective and unmanly behaviour is seen to continue.

It is unpleasing in the extreme for me to have to refer to your next contention, in what is throughout a preposterous letter. You say that 'heart beating wildly'—please dear nephew, a Newby, a relative of a publisher accustomed to dealing with the most refined and discriminating of authors, should not deal so freely in cliché—you say you 'groped your way towards a narrow truckle bed and as if drugged fell into a heavy sleep'. (I make no comment here: I do not trade in the obvious.) Then, in your own unappealing terminology, 'worse was to come'. I hesitate to repeat to you the unsavoury assertions which follow, here: only the hope that the perusal of your own words may give you pause for thought, leads me to believe that you may learn to improve your ways, and this sooner rather than at a later date.

I shall go on, for this reason alone. 'I woke when the church clock, as I assumed it must be, began to chime', you write, 'and as I counted to midnight I realised I was awake and seeing in the New Year in the most ghastly and intolerable way ever devised—if devised it was. For surely, what now took place was the work of an evil prankster; one who knew I lacked light in that dreadful little cell of a room and thus could assume any shape, in my fearful imagination, that it pleased?

'Uncle'—you continued, praying I daresay for my belief in this nonsense and thus for a reprieve from my inevitable wrath at the incompetence you have shown—'Uncle, the dank creature which now lay beside me on that narrow bed was more horrible by far than the hand at the window—more shattering to the heart and soul than any monster dreamed by a child. For what lay beside me was a woman—not long dead as I soon saw when the moon looked in through the lattice with a harsh light—a woman who clung to me with the piteous desperation of one who dreads a certain return to the tomb. She asked me to save her: I swear she did; but my arms were as heavy as lead; and she died a second time beside me there, her skin giving out a chill impossible either to forget or to describe.

'I have had horrors, Uncle, pray forgive and understand me in my hour of need.

'I lay all the remainder of the night while the moon played catch-as-catch-can with the black clouds that trailed the night sky. I froze; my teeth chattered; and when the handle of the bedroom door began to turn I almost wept with relief that someone—Tabby, perhaps; I did not even care if it was the Reverend Brontë himself—had come to assuage my fears. But the turning of the handle was ghostly, too, Uncle, I give you my word it was. 'Emily!' came a voice from the passage: a high, squeaky voice, yet the door did not open and my dead bed-companion did not move an inch. 'Emily' —that is all it said: oh Uncle, do believe me now!'

Henry, I shall terminate this letter to you with a few words of advice. First, you must expunge from your mind instantly all thoughts of that night at Haworth Parsonage. I believe you were not, as you had at first suspected, the victim of a prankster, but instead the innocent recipient of a potion or dangerous drug administered to you earlier. (The good Tabby had left a carafe of water in the room, I daresay: in your fevered condition you drank some, and hallucinated the rest.) There was no hand at the window; no squeaky-voiced supplicant at the bedroom door; and, most worthy of all to remember, no one whatever in your bed.

I am interested, however, by your description of the early hours of January 1st in this year of Our

Lord, 1849. You stated that it 'brought a sense of returning sanity' to pull out the contents of the bag of snippets found under the rug in the downstairs study. 'I had been with people from another, terrible world, all night', you write, 'and to read of the exploits of mortals, wicked though they may be— and I speak, naturally, of Mr Heathcliff, of whom I informed you earlier, Uncle—is infinitely better than to be closeted with the dead.

'So'—as you concluded your (now-destroyed) missive to me, nephew—'I grasped the pages which spilled readily into my hands as dawn broke. Nobody stirred in the house, and if the dog Keeper barked or howled from time to time, I was happy to remind myself that, for all the hound's ferocity, it was, like myself, a hot-blooded thing.

'I knew where I was in the strange story I had begun to read earlier. Mr Heathcliff, rich with his wife's fortune, was making his way back to England to reclaim his lost love, Cathy. I tremble to confess this, but I had a wish to read more of this lovely girl, this free, wild spirit. I could feel for Heathcliff, even, in his passion for his childhood sweetheart.

'Yet what I read shocked me, Uncle. You ask me to send you the pages I have read so far. But I cannot.'

Henry, I conclude this communication to you with an order, *which cannot be disobeyed*, to send the pages you are reading to me directly in London.

I have written to ask you for these when your letters of January 3rd and 4th arrived here and am most surprised and disappointed to have received nothing from you to date.

Yours in anticipation
    Thomas Cautley Newby
        Mortimer St, off Cavendish Square

EDITOR'S NOTE

It is with regret that we pronounce ourselves baffled and frustrated by the terror which appears to have afflicted Henry Newby ever since his unfortunate visit to Haworth Parsonage. We must, sadly, date his apparent inability to distinguish the true from the false, the real from the fictional, one might say, from this time. Did Newby perhaps fancy himself a successor to Lockwood, the traveller whose cold and other chest symptoms kept him so conveniently in bed while Nelly Dean recounted the tale of passion that was Heathcliff and Cathy? Was Newby, in fact, as much a story-teller as a reader of tall tales? We cannot know.

CHAPTER FIVE

THE DEPOSITION OF HENRY NEWBY

The words which follow here, being of a confidential nature, shall not leave my safe keeping. They shall not be posted to London as my uncle demands; and they shall be shown to no-body. It comes as no surprise to this reader that the pages had been intended for burning— and I make this deposition for the purpose of announcing that when they have been read they will be incinerated and never referred to more. Meanwhile, I hereby declare that the search for the missing manuscript, a mission which has at least acquainted me with the power of the word, is at an end. The house stirs and someone, doubtless Tabby or the woman referred to last night as 'Miss Charlotte', can be heard moving about: a poker riddles the grate in what I assume to be the 'downstairs study', directly below; curtains are drawn back. But before I slip from the window of the tiny room I have occupied for what seems an age—since last year, one might say, as the year of our Lord 1849 has come in since I entered it —I must finish my perusal of this confession by a madman and (it seems) a murderer, a being for whom I have nevertheless the deepest sympathy and understanding.

To go back to the beginning: since first light entered this miserable cell I have been occupied in reading these

pages. My father and my brothers would be astonished to
find me so engaged. But, as I stated previously, a record
of the pain and ecstasy of a living being is preferable by
far to the blank page presented by the dead. If I am to be
haunted, it will be by a man who has fought for his life
and for the recognition of his humanity all his days, a
man who knows passion as few possibly could; and whose
need for revenge is as urgent as the demands addressed
by a parched throat to the desert. Mr Heathcliff—for it is
he who recounts his life to Mr Lockwood still—is in his
upper room at The Heights, a room not unlike the chamber where I find myself today. Oh, if I could only have
known Mr Lockwood!—but his pages are dated 1802
and Mr Lockwood, should he be alive still, would very
likely have forgotten the import and even the content of
his visit there, close on half a century ago. I tremble to
think of Mr Lockwood's state of mind when, on returning to his lodgings, he sought to write down the story of
Mr Heathcliff—particularly, one might say, when his
lodgings, supervised by the good Ellen Dean, were lo-
cated in Thrushcross Grange. Poor Mr Lockwood, seated
(as I envisage him) at the desk lately occupied by Mr
Edgar Linton, must have realised, even as he wrote, that
Mrs Linton (that is, Cathy, Mr Heathcliff's undying passion) had lain on her deathbed just above him, in the scar-
let and white drawing-room. He would have been inhuman if he had not thought he heard cries of love and
yearning emanating from that chamber.

But I have been transported out of myself in a manner unsuitable for the writing of this Deposition. I wish
merely to transcribe what I have found; to leave for posterity a record of what I have had before my eyes today.
Whether the account of the early life of this strange, in-
scrutable man, ageing and resigned to his own coming
death on the occasion of Mr Lockwood's last visit to The
Heights, will provide the key to his nature, we may never

know. But, for the future interest of those who visit the now uninhabited dwelling 'The Withens', this account supplies a summation, at the least, of the sufferings endured by an unwanted and abandoned child in the last third of the past century. And I conclude that it is in order for us to congratulate ourselves, as a nation, on the progress we have made, both in ensuring the passing of laws to abolish slavery and in the growth of charitable foundations and the like—the latter a lifetime's interest of my dear mother, the late Mrs Eileen Newby.

oઢ

'My first memory'—*here Heathcliff continues to Mr Lockwood*—'is of the ship that bore me from a country where it was white with snow nearly all year round, and people went into the long hut on hands and knees—although I, being no more than three or four years old, could walk in with them upright. I remember we ate fish, and I would dig holes in the ice to catch them; and at one time I had an eel between my teeth and a fish in either hand; though I had to run up a tree, which I could do with ease even at that age, to escape those who wanted to seize them from me.

'When the ship came in, I was dragged to the far end of the hut and black paint was put on me, covering my whole body. People were laughing; and the disguise was a caprice of the Captain or of someone who wished to sell me as a slave when once we reached the West Indies.

'For this was where we were bound, in the great ship. As we sailed into warm seas I made a friend of a Negro boy, who had come over from an island in the West Indies and was now taken back there, to go into slavery also. We used to make signs with our hands to each other, for we knew nothing of each other's language. At first, my friend the Negro lad would take my hands

and spread my fingers out, to stare at them in amaze-
ment. For it was true that my thumb and first finger were
longer by far than his, or anyone else's on board ship. This
came from climbing the trees and grasping the branches,
which I had learned to do even when they were slippery
with ice and snow.

'As the sky grew blue and the seas warm, my companion the Negro boy grew excited at the return to his
native island of St Lucia, in the Windward Islands south
of America. But I wanted only to swim in cold water; even
when we docked in the busy harbour at Soufrières and
went round by canoe to the shore where people were to
be judged and sold, I felt no sense of belonging in this
landscape. The sad palm trees I had no wish to run up,
for I knew I would find myself stranded, once there,
amongst the spiky fronds at the top.

'You may understand, Mr Lockwood, why my visit
to this island—and to this dreadful shore, with my late
wife Louisa—brought me little but alarm, even a sense of
persecution. How had I come to find myself in the place
I had been brought to as a child, barely old enough to
care for myself? What evil star had dictated my return to
the very coast I had fled?

'It may be that I shall never know the answer. But
on this second occasion of coming to the wild and law-
less area that forms the southern part of the island of St
Lucia, I remembered with the vividness of a dream the
day when, as a child without language, family or hope, I
ran off into the rainforest and lived there days and nights
before a passing huntsman found me and smuggled me
on board a ship to England. I remember the bright birds,
no bigger than a glance from beneath the eyelashes of a
courtesan's painted eye; and I recall the monsters, igua-
nas I daresay they may have been, which glared at me
once night fell, their green orbs flickering on and off until
I thought I would go mad at their determination and

regularity. Most of all, I thought then very fondly of the man who rescued me from this island I knew I would hate, but with a familiarity I have since learnt belongs to a dread of kin—for I had none, and could not explain my aversion to the place.

'My saviour, a man who had no fear of capture (and I heard it said of him when once we arrived at the harbour that it was he who, as chief of these Caribee people, decided on which of his fellow islanders would be saved and which sent to almost certain death on the stifling slave-ships) carried me aboard a vessel bound for the cold waters I pined for. He showed neither fear nor haste in depositing me with the Captain's mate, and, treated like a pet monkey by the crew, I sailed to Liverpool in safety.

'Mr Lockwood, there are times in life when self-sufficiency is all. I found this when taken in by a family of Scots who beat and starved me, making of me a servant, worse than the slave I would have been if I had suffered transportation to the sugar cane fields of Antigua, as so many of the other conscripts had been. I was far from the long hut and the clean, pure snow I had known; remaining unaddressed in human language and knowing only the voice of a leather strap descending on my back or the sentence of a shoe stamping on my sleeping body to rouse me for another day of labour. I was as wordless as I had been when first captured and taken out to the West Indies.

'I ran away with the assistance of the dog this grim family kept chained night and day in all weathers, out in their yard. The beast, as ferocious to me as to any other stranger at first, soon grew to understand I was as capable of violent reminders of the laws it had been trained to obey as were its owners; it grew, grudgingly enough, I admit, to respect me; and once I had begun to add the odd morsel of beef gristle or fat to its daily oatmeal mess, it positively slavered with love each time I came out into the back quarters of the house.

'One night I let the animal loose. Mad with joy, it bounded right out into the street, and as it was clear where my duty lay, I rushed after it. One of the family's waggons (they imported and exported grain) was being loaded up, and I jumped in under the canopy, the dog after me. I was free: I shall never forget the excitement of that day; and as I realised we were going north—to the family's Glasgow warehouse, I suppose—I sniffed the air and breathed the ice and snow I had known in the country of my first home. With the dog quivering beside me, I slept and woke on the long journey; and it was only when the waggon-driver grew suspicious on a halt in the green hills by a long loch deep and dark as the seas where I had fished in my extreme youth, that I decided it was best to depart before being hauled by the scruff of the neck back to Liverpool. The dog, for all that I tried to deter it, leapt from the waggon; and we would have been discovered together by virtue of the grain that dropped from my ragged clothing, if the hound, as in the fairy-tale of Hansel and Gretel, had not devoured each one as we went.

'You may ask, Mr Lockwood, how I came to be acquainted even with the notion of a fairy-tale, brought up as I was without any way of understanding the words people spoke to each other or the fancy tales they liked to tell.

'This I can answer: one good man, a philanthropist whose memory can never be erased from my conscious mind, saved this poor orphan from continuing ignorance and deprivation. One man, who found me wandering in the streets of Liverpool—for the waggoner, seeing his store of grain disturbed, went after me with his apprentice, and for all my efforts I was caught, along with the limping beast I had brought with me, and returned to the hated city—one man, as if sent to me by the angels, changed my life forever.

'This emissary from a Heaven of which I had never been informed, took me into his care and we walked together to his house, one day's journey by foot to the moors above Gimmerton.

'Yes, Mr Lockwood, my rescuer's name was Joseph Earnshaw, God rest his soul.

'So why, you say to me, did you not learn to believe in goodness, to trust in the Lord and the rest?

'The answer to this is as sad as it is inevitable.

'I found the love of my life in the house where I was taken by this good-hearted man. Her name was Cathy. And while I taught her the love of freedom, she instructed me in the art of joy.

'But her brother, heir to the house where I had at first been treated as a member of the family, came to hate me and to plot my murder at each turn. I was ignored, reduced to a stable lad, despised and overlooked by all.

'And one day, I stood by the stable door and heard Cathy in the kitchen, informing Nelly Dean the housekeeper that she could never marry me—it would degrade her to do so. Cathy loved that milksop Edgar Linton, and would marry him. So, once again, I fled. And three years later, rich and admired, I made my return.'

CHAPTER *SIX*

THE DEPOSITION OF HENRY NEWBY

By the time I had read these pages; had suffered for Mr Heathcliff on his return from the far side of the world, a fortune to his name and yet no prospect of a bride—for his Cathy, 'my Cathy' as I am by now inclined to consider the wild, free spirit formed, as he was, by moor and storm, by a love of liberty and a hatred for the conventions of the world, had married Edgar Linton and could never be his—by the time, as I say, I had wept for each one of the separated couple and had dried my tears sufficient for a descent into the hall of the Parsonage, it was well past midday.

For all that, no one stirred. The door into the kitchen was open, and a lack of bustle, augmented by a chill such as I had seldom experienced in a house where access to the outside is barred by a stout oak door and windows are well covered with curtains of a heavy velvet, worn with age but excluding draughts with much the same determination as when, one must suppose, the Reverend Brontë had come to take up his living there some thirty years before, came out into the hall to greet me. It was evident that the stove was unlit; and had been so all night, causing the glacial temperature which prevailed throughout the building. It was evident, also, that no human being could have sustained such a cold, all night through. The only hope, as one might term it, for the survival of any member of the family or staff at Haworth, lay in the study, the door of which was firmly closed. I had, as may be imagined, no desire to try the handle: I knew the key was on the inside; and furthermore, I had absolutely no wish to find my host, the good parson of this small community, in the process of warming himself at a blaze kindled with more of the precious papers which made up the account I now read. What if the further exploits of Mr Heathcliff, an evil man perhaps, but one as blisteringly honest as any mortal born in this age of sin could ever show himself to be, were at that very moment affording solace to the Rector of Haworth as he snoozed before the flames? It was too horrible to think of. I would then never know what became of this benighted soul—or whether his great passion—to be blunt, as I must learn to be, for I know now that my vocation is as a writer, not a servant of the law—was ever consummated. Did Mr Brontë, to follow the metaphor (if this is indeed what it may be) warm his toes in the embers of Heathcliff's undying love?

I did not go into the study. I had a good number of pages still in the bag I had slid from under the rag rug earlier and must pray to God that Tabby had chosen one of Mr Brontë's sermons, rather than the confessions of this surely justified sinner, to light the study fire. But where was Tabby? Where was the 'Miss Charlotte' I had heard speaking the evening before? Was I left alone, in this unearthly coldness, with a holy man and the shadow of last night's companion, a nightmare or a ghost? And if so, was the gaunt vicar of New Year's Eve as much a phantasm as the rest?

Thoughts such as these drove me to the front door; and once I had stepped out into the crisp air of a January day I regretted my folly and excitability at the notions I had entertained when under the roof of Haworth Parsonage. I had come already apprehensive at my Uncle's displeasure if I should fail, to seek a manuscript by an author, and had mistaken the address—that was all. No Mr Ellis Bell resided now—or had ever resided—at the Parsonage. I had instead stumbled on an eccentric family, whose members included the devilish Mr Heathcliff, and I had come on his memoir. That it had alarmed me —had, even, changed my way of observing life—could not be denied. But otherwise my nerves alone accounted for the supposition that a dead woman had lain beside me last night. It had been no more than a twisted sheet on a damp bed. Faulty plumbing accounted for the high-pitched tones of what I had thought to be a supernatural visitor beyond the door. The truth was now clear to me —I had been drawn too deeply into a world never before glimpsed or heard—to understand the effect wrought on me. It was little wonder, I could not refrain all the same from concluding that all traces of the ungodly were swept under the carpet, here; and I felt shame—if, also a measure of excitement—at having read the life story of one the parson's family can no longer, for reasons of respectability and virtue, claim as kin.

EDITOR'S NOTE

The pages presented here comprise the cache found at auction recently, the surprise in the whole endeavour consisting of the finding of a further bundle of papers tucked into the packet containing Mr Newby's deposition, as well as the confession—so we must imagine—of the origins of Heathcliff, as written shortly before her death in December 1848 by Emily Brontë. We had hoped, naturally, for elucidation on the 'missing' parts of the original second novel; and had considered ourselves fortunate indeed in our quest for answers to two of literature's most pressing and perplexing questions, viz. did Heathcliff and Cathy in fact consummate their passion, and was young Cathy therefore the daughter not of Edgar Linton but of Heathcliff?—and, to solve the riddle of Hindley Earnshaw's being found dead at Wuthering Heights six months after the death in childbirth of his sister, did Heathcliff in fact murder him? We had supposed, once poor Henry Newby became aware of his hero's fictional nature, that he would not be deterred from reading—and relaying to his uncle, his journal, or even to posterity—the next chapters in the story he had failed to understand was the very manuscript the unscrupulous publisher Thomas Cautley Newby had sent him to retrieve from Haworth. It would be normal, as our colleagues at the Brontë Museum agree, to wish to pursue the tale confided by a rogue such as Heathcliff; and Newby's abrupt loss of interest is hard to understand. We can only hope that further searches and enquiries will yield the rest. Meanwhile, our conclusion must be that real life and real people—such as Wuthering Heights and its denizens were assumed by young Mr Newby to be—were already of greater interest to the reader in the mid nineteenth century, than novels; and for this insight we are grateful. It is not only today, we are now in a position to emphasise, that biography holds the whip hand in book store and library alike.

The further bundle of papers referred to earlier appeared at first to be of interest only by reason of its proximity to the Brontë material (if such Henry Newby's discovery beneath the rag rug in the parsonage library, will turn out to be. Forensic experts work now on tracing the script, thought to be nearer to that of Branwell Brontë than his sister: results will be confirmed later this week).

Without—we trust—suffering from the naivety of poor Henry Newby, we read the pages, and present a portion of them below, for further study and comment.

CHAPTER SEVEN

THE STATEMENT OF CECILY WOODHOUSE

On New Year's Day 1849 Mr Henry Newby came to my house in Haworth and demanded assistance.

It was just beginning to snow when he arrived on my doorstep. I had seen him, naturally, from the window of the parlour.

I have lived at Northfield Farm for over twenty years, my husband being a hill farmer and his father before him. I go very seldom to visit my relatives at Gimmerton. In summer there's too much work in the fields, and in winter a fog comes down, or else snow such as we saw on New Year's Day, when a good five feet fell and we had a dozen or so sheep buried and beyond rescue by our collie dog.

When I last went across the moor, it was on a day in late spring and I picked a bunch of harebells for my nan, old Mrs Dean as they call her, who is at a cottage by The Grange. There's a great-nephew who comes from Halifax to see the old lady from time to time, but his wife died and I'm told he remarried and went south. He is related on Mr Dean's side; Mr Dean who was stepbrother to my grandmother, that is. There are a good many families around here who are difficult to puzzle out, such a time they've been closed in a valley together.

So the first big flakes of snow fell as this young man came down the street on the hill from the Parsonage, and then stopped outside our house. I would say he looked pale, or the like—but he didn't strike me as poorly. When I opened the door at his knock, though, he half fell into our hall, and then burst out crying like a baby. I had to take him into the kitchen, and mop his face and pour boiling water out of the kettle for a pot of tea. Then I offered him a bowl of porridge and he wolfed it down without waiting for milk on the oats. It occurred to me he was a prisoner on the run—and I made sure my carving knife was within range. Not that this one had the strength to hurt a fly, but you never know if they're wrong in the head.

When he could talk, our visitor spent a long time apologising for the state he was in. He'd been sent on a mission by his uncle—a man who was famous down in London, so he kept saying—though I don't know what difference it would have made to me if he was the King. 'I was asked', says this young man who told me to call him Henry—he was a Leeds lad, so I learnt, though you couldn't tell from his voice, it was very high-class and he spoke as if there were balls of fluff in his throat as well as his nose—'I was asked to fetch a . . . a batch of papers', and he looked hard at me then. 'I was to go to the Parsonage and find a Mr Ellis Bell. I was to collect his second book, so my uncle wrote to me. And once I was there, I found myself in a . . .' and here I had to burst out laughing at the way my new caller did indeed go pale: he's a gingery man but he looked as if a sack of flour had been emptied over him. Except for his Adam's apple, which was red as a cherry as it waggled up and down.

'Mr Newby!' I said—for I had no intention of calling him Henry. I was impatient too, by then, to get on with the supper. With snow coming down like this, Jack and the other men would be down from the hill shortly.

'I ask only if you can direct me to the proper house for Mr Bell', the newcomer went on. And his colour did recover a little, when a sound could be heard outside the kitchen—perhaps he found me taciturn and thought he'd get further with someone else.

I confess I didn't know what to reply, in the brief time I had. The arrival of the dog at the back door—for that had been the sound outside—meant Jack was half way down the home field. I'd need a tub of hot water, I could tell; the snowstorm would have started earlier, as it always does up on the Crag, and there'd be three men to dry, inside and out. All the same, I felt sorry for this visitor who was as ignorant of the events at the Parsonage, I could tell, as if he had come from the city he boasted of where his uncle lives. If it hadn't been for the dog pushing open the kitchen door I'd have stood there a few minutes longer and told Mr Newby where he could find Ellis Bell. But as it was, the black and tan collie (dripping wet and still with snow stuck to his coat) came running and snuffling up to us. 'Down', I said. 'You're soaking the both of us, Heathcliff. Out to the pantry with you'—and I delivered a kick which sent the animal cowering. 'Excuse me, Mr Newby. You don't need a wetting before you set out on your way back to Leeds tonight.'

Now I suppose I knew there was no chance of this young man finding his way home in conditions like these. The coach wouldn't leave today, and no one in their right senses would take a horse and ride across the moor: even a grown, sensible man would be taking his life in his hands if he did so. And it was pretty clear to me by now that Mr Henry Newby could not be described as being in his right mind—indeed, in the last minute or two he seemed to have lost his mind altogether. With tea and porridge inside him, this was a bad sign; and I have to say I backed off to the dresser and laid my hand on the long knife. I could hear Jack stamping snow from his

shoes by the back door and even the sound of him blow-
ing on his fingers, which generally grates on my nerves,
was welcome to me then. 'Why do you call the dog by
that name?' my strange visitor insisted. He made to move
towards me and then went back to stand by the kitchen
table and stare at nothing, as if he had just seen a ghost.

Now it is late at night and while I have time I shall
try to finish what I remember of that New Year's Day, all
of ten years ago by now.

I can't say I know now any better than I did then,
what prompted me to pull the stranger up the stairs and
hide him in the box bed in our room up there where my
sister stays on her infrequent visits from Gimmerton.
Many's the story I've heard from behind that gingham
curtain when it's pulled across to deflect the draughts
that blow in ferociously from our loft. Often I've heard
stories I'd have thought impossible, when my Nelly remembered them—but then, she was the one named after
our grandmother, and it was to her that Grandma Dean
used to tell of wild happenings and dreadful hauntings,
all when little Ellen was no more than three or four years
old.

This time, though, it was my turn to speak. I felt
sorry for the young man—there was something child-
like about him, as if he'd never been told a bedtime story
and knew he was lacking something in his life—and it
was clear, too, that this lad who spoke of London and an
uncle in such an important way, couldn't tell what was
real from the most fantastic fabrication any of his uncle's
famous authors might choose to spin.

I let Jack stump into the kitchen below with the
other shepherds and I heard him grunt at the sight of the
stew in the pot before the door closed and we were left in
silence. Apart, that is, from the sound of the hailstones
that came down as an interruption to the snow, from

time to time. And then my guest in the box bed would jump out of his skin and demand to know who was there, as the balls of ice hit our roof with a sound like an escaped felon who's climbed up there and insists on being let in. 'It's nothing, Mr Newby. Keep still, and keep your voice down as well, and I'll tell you more of the family at the Parsonage where you spent such a lively night', I said. And that would quieten him: still very white in the face, this poor fellow would poke his head out from behind the curtain and demand to know more of the man he had encountered in the hall as another year came in: where was his wife? Were there children? Did I know Tabby?—for I saw he placed me, a farmer's wife, on a level with a servant, as a townsman will.

'The Reverend Patrick Brontë', I said, when my visitor had fallen back in the box bed again—I didn't want Jack climbing the stairs and finding a strange man conversing with his wife and visible for all to see. 'Patrick Brontë's wife died, God bless her soul, after giving birth to five daughters and a son. She is buried in Haworth churchyard—and if you need to find out more about the family, you'll discover a number of them under the turf there with her, a good many taken before their time.'

And so I went on, as young Newby stared up at me as if I gave sustenance simply by filling him in on the people who had acted as invisible hosts when he paid his call at his uncle's behest to Haworth Parsonage. I told him about the saintly woman lost by the daughters to the family disease of consumption; of the cruel school which had claimed the lives of the two eldest girls, and how Patrick Brontë had kept Charlotte and Anne and Emily at home to be educated after that, with his wife's sister Miss Branwell in attendance.

'Branwell?' said Henry Newby, and he sat up with a jerk in his bed, so his head hit the ceiling of the wooden box bed. 'Did she speak in a high-pitched voice—did she care for a girl who died in the upper room at the Parsonage?'

'No, Master Henry', I replied—for I saw now that there had been events of the night before that were of an unusual nature, and I knew it was best, if the truth was to be extracted, with those who think themselves gentry at least, to take on the voice and manner of an old nurse or retainer. 'Aunt Branwell, as they all called her, was impartial in her care for the remaining children. Master Branwell—that was the name of the only son—well, she found it hard to like him, I'll confess. And Miss Emily after that, who had as stubborn a nature and as wild a temper as you could find', I went on, wondering what type of visitation my poor visitor had suffered. 'Especially after Miss Charlotte and Miss Anne went away to teach, that was a hard time for Miss Branwell. You'd think, with only two young ones in the house—Master Branwell and Emily, that is—that her work would be reduced. But they were up to any crazy scheme you could imagine, Mr Newby. Old Mr Brontë knew nothing of their deceivings and exploits. One day they'd be out on the moor dressed as pirates—if you can call a few old rags a true disguise—the next, Emily would have pulled one of her mother's dresses from the press on the landing and be dressed for a ball, or so she thought it, calling herself a Countess and having her hand kissed and bowed over by young Branwell. It wasn't good then, Master Henry, and no one could speak to the Reverend Brontë about it because he was off in his own imaginings, with God I daresay, though it seemed altogether stranger than that.'

A silence fell, as my guest digested some of the complexities of the family. 'So who was Mr Ellis Bell?' he asked at last, as I heard the men down below spooning in their meal, and the dog barking beyond the pantry door to be let in. 'Was he a lodger at the house?'

I'd been expecting the question so I answered with all I truly knew, unsatisfying though it must have seemed to the young man. 'The three sisters used the same name of Bell for their writings', I said. 'Miss Charlotte—that was the one you informed me earlier you'd heard speak in a loud voice on the stairs—she was the eldest and she didn't mind that they knew she was a Mr Currer Bell, though I cannot see for the life of me what good it did her to be laughed at by the county. Miss Anne didn't mind either, when the news came out. But Miss Emily—the youngest—she wanted it kept a secret, that she was Ellis Bell. Right up to the day of her death, just two weeks ago, she wanted it to be kept quiet. That'll be the reason your uncle sent you to Mr Bell, sir.'

'I see', said the young man, though just at that moment he saw nothing at all, having fallen back on his bunk, and the curtain falling closed beside him.

'Master Branwell died just three months before his sister', I went on, though I doubted whether my visitor needed any more information on the subject of the Brontë family. 'Ever since the day the moor went up—back when they were very young—they were close. She pulled him out of the bog—it was like lava, pouring down the side of the hill, and I well remember it all even now.'

There was silence from the interior of the bed. I had sent Mr Newby to sleep, so I supposed, by recounting the sad lives of those sisters in this remote place. But, as I went to pull the curtain aside, a pale hand shot out to grasp mine.

'You have neglected one person in your account, Mrs Woodhouse', came a low, urgent voice from within. 'What became of Heathcliff? I do not hear of his life or fortunes from you, madam. Is he alive but forgotten by all of you? Is that the reason for your refusal to speak of him?'

EDITOR'S NOTE

We would have liked to have had the satisfaction, here, of informing hapless readers of these 'statements', 'depositions', 'fragments' and the like, that Henry Newby's visit to Mrs Woodhouse was a fiction, possibly his first foray in the world of creative writing. Mrs Woodhouse did not exist: the budding author's imagination took over, and in his desire to portray a woman's voice and view of himself, he ran riot amongst the real inhabitants of Haworth and the fictional characters of Wuthering Heights.

This, unfortunately, can be seen not to be the case. Parish records show J. Woodhouse and his wife Cecily to have been in residence at the farmhouse on the fringes of the village in the year 1849, although Mrs Woodhouse was that year removed from the parish register. We may conclude that Henry Newby was unable to resist taking the real name of the woman whose farmhouse he visited and then, in his eagerness to revisit the novel which by now seemed so much more real to him than the mundane existence he found there, gave her as kinswoman the famous Nelly Dean.

The above led us, with the assistance of the University of York, to search for an Ellen Dean in the vicinity. Had Emily Brontë perhaps taken her moorland Scheherezade from real life? Enquiries have so far produced no answers.

CHAPTER EIGHT

THE DEPOSITION OF HENRY NEWBY

It is difficult to set down—even to recall correctly—the succession of events following the speech of the shepherd's wife on that bleak New Year's morning of 1849. There was a scuffling downstairs, followed by the dog's name bellowed out by a man as bad-tempered as might be expected after suffering a snowstorm on the hill and very probably the death of three or four of his ewes. 'Heathcliff!' the husband—as I took him to be—of my informant shouted out a few more times, the word jarring in my ears along with my own plaintive request of the good woman that she tell me the story of the man I now pitied and loved and would never scorn, for all the evil deeds laid to his name. 'Heathcliff!' shouted the farmer—and I heard the door bang out at the back and three or four others set off, whistling in long, shrill bursts to the collie, to go seek in deep drifts those members of the flock lost since the last ravages of the storm.

I decided to wait no longer. Mrs Woodhouse, as I was to discover was her name, had run from the room and down the stairs, and a fine to and fro started up, succeeded by the clatter of a spoon against a pot and a chair scraping across the flags, this joined by another.

I crept from the box bed where I had lain hidden
and made my way onto the sloping roof above the pantry, by way of a small window rimed with snow and frost
but surprisingly amenable to my thumbnail and a strong
tug when it came to be needed. I slipped and slithered
down to the ground, dislodging parcels of snow as I
went. I was able to observe, once on the ground, that the
men were a good hundred yards off, climbing the hill
with their heads bent as they searched the terrain. The
dog ran ahead of the men, stopping once to paw the snowy
hillocks and whimper, when they had got nearly to the
cairn at the summit of the hill.

I eased myself round the side of the house. However
tempted I might be to enter by the back door, I resisted
the urge. In any case, I felt no interest in looking through
the kitchen window, at the farmer and his wife at their
marital breakfast—though I did quickly glance in—for it
was the very positioning of back door, pantry, and small
stable there which drew my care and thought. Was it not
in an arrangement of buildings like these—and with
moor and hill looming beyond—that my hero Heathcliff
heard the death-dealing words of loss of love from Cathy?
Did she not proclaim to the old housekeeper, Mrs Dean,
that she would never marry a stable lad such as Heathcliff, and find herself looked down on by the world?

The old shepherd indoors must have had sufficient
of his breakfast, for he came out the back and stood puff-
ing at his pipe as the last stars faded from the sky and the
false dawn was succeeded by a stronger light of day. He
was old, I saw, as I slunk away to the side of what appeared to be a wash-house, my footsteps muffled by the
freshly fallen snow. This ancient keeper of the flock
could never have walked back up the hill, in search of
missing sheep. I wondered for a moment at his wife being so much younger—then I ran, for suddenly I was ex-
posed, once the wash-house eaves ended and my cover

was gone. I ran I had no idea where—down towards Haworth as I hoped and prayed, drawn by the idea of transport, comfort or advice as to a way out of the place. But truly I had no notion, now, of where the village with its steep cobbled street might lie.

A solitary man trudged along a track where snow had been shovelled to one side, leaving a path no wider than would allow a single file progression along it. Already a further fall needed no predicting, as the sky had turned heavy and dark; and even as I went, keeping at a discreet distance behind the walker, a whirl of snowflakes began to descend on the landscape, obliterating the bank made by a previous digger and adding to the uniform whiteness.

All the same, I walked on. The man before me appeared undeterred by the conditions—or was, perhaps, so familiar with the region that he could pay little attention to the weather. I was glad of his presence there, I confess. No lights showed anywhere; I might have been following him into the wilderness; but I was uncommonly glad not to find myself alone.

After a while, as I kept pace with the steady rhythm of my guide, a faint glow did appear on the horizon. But, unsure as to whether this was a delusion, like those said to be undergone in the desert by explorers lost and desperate for the sight of an oasis, I quenched the hope that rose in my breast and trudged on. It was this new resolve —or perhaps only the limitation of an apparently sightless man leading the way was the cause—but suddenly I found myself brought up against him. I felt my legs slide beneath me, as I tried to curb my steady and not inconsiderable speed. In short, I ran right into the back of the stranger; and, not surprisingly, he halted also and swivelled round to inspect what manner of attack he was about to undergo.

It is as difficult here to describe my sensations on seeing the unknown walker's face as it would be to set down an accurate account of leaving this life and of going to meet the denizens beyond the gates of Hell. For the character who turned and looked down at me was handsome—he was devilishly handsome, I expect some would say, yet every feature and lineament was marked —or so it seemed to me—by a profound sadness. Who was this lachrymose fiend?—for soon I saw I was right, and that he wept: tears flowed down his rugged cheeks which could not have been caused by an icy wind or a fresh fall of snow. How had he sinned?—and for what crime, if this was the case, did he repent? Or had he, as it came to me in slow degrees of horror, simply lost his heart's desire, the love of his life? Did he survive only to regret each passing day on earth? Did he exist solely to be reunited with his passion in the grave?

So I speculated, and before long there was not one trace of doubt in me that I had walked behind none other than Heathcliff. He it was who led me to the place where he had run free with his childhood sweetheart, and where he must live on in bitterness as she indulges her desire for calm and comfort with another. This man who cried so copiously, thinking himself far from prying eyes, was the man his Cathy had refused when talking to the housekeeper by the kitchen door up at The Heights. And it was to this house that I knew he must now lead me.

'Who are you?' The stranger's voice was low and gentle: I would not have imagined it to issue from such a one as Heathcliff. 'And'—for he saw by now that I had no evil intentions towards him—'you must be lost, sir. Where are you from? Where do you go?'

As he spoke, the good man—more of a saint now than a devil, I had to admit, but still as handsome as when I had first seen him, propelled me gently down a slope to the side of the now-invisible road. A light gleamed in the near-night to which this New Year's Day had, due to the gathering snow-clouds, sourly turned. My feet, I realised, as this kind stranger placed his hand on my back to guide me further in the direction of a huddle of buildings, were devoid of sensation. I shall never forget the gratitude I felt at that time, for the appearance of the man I saw as Heathcliff: he had known, somehow, of my sympathy for his sad fate, so I considered, and he had come to me like a shepherd who, after days searching in the blind whiteness of the snow, catches sight of a member of his missing flock.

That this had indeed been pure conjecture came both as a sorrow and a relief to me. The stranger, as soon as he crossed the threshold of a hostelry dimly proclaiming itself as the Black Bull on a battered sign which swung alongside a lantern, was greeted with familiarity and respect. It was soon clear that my Heathcliff's name was John Brown; references were made to recent work in the churchyard at Haworth, the chiselling of inscriptions and so on, which convinced me he must be sexton of the parish; and very soon, when I was seated in the 'snug' by a roaring fire and sipping a glass of hot brandy, I had forgotten my insistence on labelling my saviour by the name of a man I had never encountered. This had been due to hearing the dog up at the farm called for by this name, I concluded. But I was curious, I confess, to discover from the agreeable Mr Brown just what the connection could be between the man whose confession I had read just one long night ago at the Parsonage and the people hereabouts. Was Heathcliff, like Mr Bony, the Napoleon of popular nightmare, a bogeyman for the district? Where did he reside now, if still living? All this I determined to ask the good sexton when he returned from his conversation at a table with friends and companions and resumed the seat next to me, on the wooden bench by the fire.

As it transpired, my new friend John Brown had many to visit on this bleak morning of 1st January last; and soon I desisted from following his progress round the room, a sense of tact and discretion preventing me from attempting to overhear the murmured expressions of grief—and, so it seemed—condolence, both given and received by the good sexton. There was a predominance of the mention of 'Master Branwell'—that I will say— and on each occasion the sad demise of the son of that cavernous Reverend Brontë whom I had met briefly at the Parsonage was mentioned, poor Mr Brown wiped away a tear. But the name of 'Miss Emily', said with an altogether different and cautious-sounding ring, was, to my mind at least, the more affecting of the two recent bereavements suffered by the people of Haworth. I took the opportunity, therefore, when approached by the host and asked in the blunt tones so different from those of my native Leeds, if I desired more of the hot brandy, to double my order in the hope of obtaining further inform- ation on this curious and perplexing family.

'He would sit where you are now', the landlord as- sured me, once the strong liquor, as fiery to touch and to stomach as any beverage served in the infernal regions could be; 'Master Branwell would take as much as you, sir, and three times over, before it was time for him to find his way back to the Parsonage. It was impossible, on occasion, for the climb to be attempted. But you know all that, sir, I have no doubt. For all his oddities—and I believe I've seen a whole world slumbering in the eyes of that man, a country known only to himself and his sister—'

'Yes', chipped in a man who moved from his pew and came to join me in the 'snug', a tankard of ale in his hand. 'She had the patience, and he was blessed by good fortune to have a woman who'd carry him up to bed. Everyone said that. She'd wait up for him half the night,

Miss Emily, for fear the parson would come to know of Master Branwell's drinking. Yet they say, on the day he died, he rose to his feet when Mr Brontë entered the room and then he fell dead.'

'And what world did you see in Branwell Brontë?' I enquired of my host once our new companion had buried his lower face in his ale. I had the impression the poetic sensibilities of the Black Bull's proprietor would yield more than the prosaic delivery of the beer-drinker; though in this, as in so many other assumptions made at this time I was, as I must confess, completely in error.

'Oh, they whispered their plots and stories', the publican confided, his excitement subsiding as he came to realise—or so it appeared clear—that the content of these 'plots' and stories were completely unknown to him. 'She lasted only three months after he went, Mr—' And I saw that my imaginative host, still filled with the spirits of the New Year's Eve which had gone before, now tried to dampen his own while searching for some reassurance on the subject of my reliability.

'I was asked by my uncle, the London publisher Thomas Cautley Newby', I began, aware I sounded pompous; and at once I knew myself rewarded by looks of ill-disguised merriment from others at tables in the inn. 'I am in search of a manuscript written by a Mr Ellis Bell —or, as I am informed, a Miss Emily—'

'Master Branwell, he was writing when he died', vouchsafed the ale-imbiber, his upper lip now adorned with a white foam. 'His sister cared for him when he was poorly, she'd do anything for him. She had a temper on her, though: she'd beat her dog half to death, would Emily'.

The landlord left us at this point; and John Brown came to sit by us, just as I had hoped to pursue my investigations. I had not thought before that I would regret the arrival of the sexton, when I had looked forward so keenly to speaking with him, and to thanking him for acting as my guide through the snow, even if he had not been conscious at the time of his kind actions. Now, however, I felt I'd more to gain from filling the now-empty tankard held aloft by my new friend; and once my offer had been accepted and he had gone off from the 'snug' to be replenished, I turned to Mr Brown for a brief exchange before my informant's return. Something told me, I should say, that scandal or a secret of some kind lurked here at the Black Bull, and the sexton, mistakenly assumed at first by myself to be as outspoken or brutally frank a man as Heathcliff, would prove the last being on earth to confide it. In this, at least, I found I was correct in my assumptions.

'No', said the handsome sexton, shaking his head firmly when I enquired whether Mr Branwell and Miss Emily Brontë had indeed 'plotted' in some way against others—maybe against members of their own family, when they had been still children, with unpleasant consequences. 'No, Mr Newby'—for he had heard my name, and at least, as I noted with some satisfaction, spoke it respectfully. 'There was a time when the two were together without their siblings, at the Parsonage. The sisters had gone off to teach, or were at school. There were—' and here John frowned, while searching for the word. 'There were intimations that the works of a poet who lived far from God influenced their thinking, for they spoke to each other in a way that was, for that brief time, quite dissimilar from their previous allusions or way of speaking.'

'And who was that?' I enquired, not wishing to show my sense of sudden regret at the absence of knowledge on the subject of poets or other literary matters. 'You intrigue me, Mr Brown.'

But at that moment the beer-drinker reappeared, brimming tankard in hand, and joined us on the wooden bench, while the landlord came forward with an armful of stout logs and piled them on the fire. 'If you wish to know my opinion', said the man with his mug of ale, once a long draught had been taken and the foam had risen up his cheeks again, 'they each said they wrote books —but it was he who showed me a letter that proves he was the writer, out of the two of them'.

'And what letter is that?' asked John Brown in icy tones, before I could discover more on the subject of the brother and sister so recently interred in the churchyard adjacent to the Parsonage. 'I would thank you—'and here the mild-mannered sexton positively glowered at the man who buried himself once more in his beer—'I would be glad if you would not confuse matters so indiscreetly, Sam'.

At this, and in response to a New Year's greeting called out by an arrival at the Black Bull, a jovial-looking man with a younger companion, the sexton rose and hurried away to return the season's good wishes. My new friend—if I may call him such: perhaps all new friends start as appearing to be inveterate gossips and gain our affection that way—leant towards me on the bench. His beer breath came strong at me; but I did not shrink from him, for a bundle of papers was fished from the depths of his coat and pushed across the table towards me. By a miracle—for so I was to consider it later—no one saw the transaction, and the sheaf of closely written pages was transferred to my bag while the inn-keeper served those who had just come in, and the other patrons of the Black Bull entered some kind of singing which took up

every scrap of their energies. 'The letter is from Heathcliff', said my supplier (for such he was, of the most pow-
erful substance I had tasted, that of the written word). 'I
heard you when you came in here asking Mr Brown if he
should be Mr Heathcliff—and I am here to inform you
that I understood the jest, sir—Mr Brown was indeed a
friend to Mr Branwell, and Mr Branwell it was, who gave
me this.'

EDITOR'S NOTE

The authorship of the following 'letter to Mr Lockwood' has become the subject of considerable controversy worldwide (in academic circles, that is: the 'man on the Clapham Omnibus', should such a being continue to exist, has little interest in the hand wielding this particular pen. Celebrities rule the book world these days, so it is widely believed).

To us, however, the fact that the script closely resembles that of Branwell Brontë is of enduring fascination. If Branwell was the author of this 'letter', is it proof of his identification with Heathcliff? If this is the case, did the drunken failure in whom the family placed all their hopes, entertain a passion for his sister Emily which sparked the incestuous love (for many considered Heathcliff to have been old Earnshaw's son) between that devil and Cathy? This possibility has been ignored in recent biographies of the poet and author of Wuthering Heights, *but we feel duty bound to record it here.*

CHAPTER NINE

Dear Mr Lockwood . . . the letter began. (Apart from a date, 1802, scrawled in a shaky hand at the top of the page, there was no indication of the provenance of the missive.)

. . . I awaited your visit when spring came this year—which will, I have no doubt, be my last. Do not grieve for me, for I rejoice at leaving a world so long without life, where the moor is dead without the sound of her step or her voice, and where the only spot I care to visit is the quiet hillside where she lies asleep.

I write because I must tell you of my return from the West Indies and what I found here when I came.

I had hopes—more than hopes: you might say expectations—of finding myself welcomed with a passion all the more ardent for having waited three long years for my reunion with Cathy. I left the docks at Liverpool a rich man—where a poor stable lad had embarked all that time ago. I disembarked with the means to make my wife blaze with the gold and jewels, the rubies and fine gowns to render her the most admired and envied woman in the country. That Cathy wished for none of these I knew well; but I had resolved in advance that she should flaunt my wealth occasionally, if only to remind the world that she had married a man of substantial means, who housed her like the queen she has always shown herself to be.

Yes, I expected her to marry me. I saw her—as I did a hundred times a day—standing in the kitchen with the old housekeeper you know well, Mr Lockwood, and this time, seeing me lurking in the gloom outside, she would run to the door and hold out her hand to me and we would fall into each others' arms. It was all a foolish mistake: I heard her say this a hundred times also—she had jested, she had no love for the weakling Edgar Linton, and had never loved anyone but me. Well, you must know the outcome of my own foolish dreams by now, Mr Lockwood—you will have heard the story from Nelly Dean. And all the county knows, with a quarter of a century gone by, how Miss Catherine Earnshaw did not wait for the lowly labourer (as her brother Hindley had made of me, but more of that later: too much, even, I daresay). Miss Earnshaw was not to be Mrs Heathcliff—and even as I write this to you after such an expanse of time, my hand curls around my pen and lifts it to the ceiling, before crashing down on table, paper and inkwells, so hard is it to rein in the rage and bafflement felt then and remembered just as vividly today. Miss Earnshaw had already, as I learned from the jeers of her odious brother, married Mr Linton and was ensconced, with all the comforts a gentleman can provide for his bride, at Thrushcross Grange.

It was dark and a moonless night, and I had travelled the best part of three thousand miles to arrive at the home I had always dreamed would one day be mine and hers. I had plans to offer a large slice of my fortune to Hindley, to give up his ownership of The Heights in favour of one who knew each mile of heather and bogland and mossy turf like the back of his hand. How unlike we were! For Master Hindley Earnshaw, who had gone deep into his drinking habits before I left for the Americas, would by the time of my return hardly be able to leave the house without stumbling and finding himself lost in a ditch or beck quite unfamiliar to him. Whereas the one who held the house in his heart and loved it with the same attention and care as did his beloved Cathy—was, Mr Lockwood, none other than the orphan brought back from Liverpool by old Mr Earnshaw and loved in turn by the old man over and above his own son. It was I, Heathcliff, who had the right to old Joseph Earnshaw's home —and to his daughter, too. She loved me. We had grown together like stalks of bracken on the moor: twined, inseparable.

Hindley leaned from an upper window of The Heights and laughed when he saw me standing there. The kitchen was in darkness; I had sensed already the absence of my love, the light of my life, my darling Cathy. I knew from the desolate air of the building that this was now no more than a drunkard's house; a drunkard no one would visit or care for. And in that instant, as he laughed down at me, I resolved to kill Hindley Earnshaw. If I had lost Cathy—and I knew, from the air of desuetude and solitary despair about the place that she had been long gone from home—I would take The Heights. And, once the vile Earnshaw's words confirmed a truth I still cannot bear to write or hear, that 'Mrs Edgar Linton' could be found at The Grange—though, he added still laughing, he doubted they would receive one such as me—I determined on becoming the owner of that estate also. Not much time elapsed, Mr Lockwood, before I had scanned the horizon for other ways to inflict damage on Mr Linton and his family—and shortly, when I have recovered strength, I shall outline to you the terrible revenge exacted on Mr Linton's house and those who lived within. For the moment, think only of me as I walked back across the moor to Gimmerton, and sought lodging as any poor vagrant might, hoping for shelter if only for the dark hours which still remained. Gone were the exalted dreams of joyful return, of compliments and vows exchanged. Like any wandering mendicant, I went knocking on an almshouse door.

CHAPTER TEN

THE DEPOSITION OF HENRY NEWBY

Heathcliff's story stopped abruptly here, a long line running across the page like a blade—or so I fancied, the very threat of murder on the part of the author seeming to take possession of me to the exclusion of any other thought.

Why had this violent, angry man stopped here?—for I saw no sign of an identical hand in any of the pages lately thrust into my grasp—what, if not his own death, could have prevented Heathcliff from going on? Had Hindley Earnshaw, a figure I now hated with all the ferocity of one who is a convert to a new faith, one in which the enemy must at all costs be eradicated from the world, found the man who dreamt of ousting him, and killed his old foe and foster-brother? If Heathcliff was indeed dead, what had been the outcome of his last message, in which he had sworn revenge on all the denizens of Thrushcross Grange? Had he succeeded in his dreadful and bloodthirsty aim: did Heathcliff writhe now in the eternal flames of Hell?

I must confess to a hope that the drunken, bullying Hindley was no longer of this world—though to imagine the two fighting in a hideous perpetuity was almost too awful to contemplate. And I must own, also, to a desire in which it is impossible to take pride: that of learning the fate of Cathy, wife of Edgar Linton, love for all time of my hero and leader, Heathcliff. Did they consummate their passion? Was the young woman who had gone impetuously to a calm existence of which she could never possibly have dreamed, so suffocated by the hypocrisies and idleness of the well-bred folk she found herself to belong to by virtue of her union with Mr Linton, that she had chosen to die along with Heathcliff? At least, in death, they would be united.

With such morbid and excited conjectures I occupied the next hour or so; and despite the cautious expression on the face of the inn-keeper when further hot brandies became necessary to me, I downed them with all the expertise, or so I persuaded myself, of the late Master Branwell. I had burning flights of the imagination, following on the sudden cessation of Heathcliff's narrative, to contend with: I understood for the first time the ecstasy and agony of the artist (for, I know not how, I learned in my inner mind that Master Branwell 'was' Heathcliff, and that his genius had brought this demonic figure to an everlasting life) and, quite literally, I worshipped the man who had brought this character into existence. I offered, as it were, a libation to the creator, the author of Heathcliff; and I began to perceive, as the Black Dog grew busier still with New Year revellers, that I could not continue with my own existence if my curiosity about the future of this momentous passion remained unsatisfied. I would—I must!—as a lover of words so *puissant* that they are indeed made flesh—hold Cathy in my arms as Heathcliff, I ardently desired, had done.

It was some minutes later, when the 'snug' had filled further and I found myself pushed up hard against a man with side-burns that resembled nothing more than carrot-tops stained green by a life passed in the damp fields and mildewed walls of a hill farm, that the horrid possibility I would never know what took place next came in to my mind. Branwell Brontë was dead: I had been told of his dreadful end only a short time ago; and his sister, devoted to the brilliant brother who provided the avid reader with the story of Heathcliff and his loves and hatreds, had followed him to the grave. I would never know—it was unbearable to contemplate, and the realisation had me calling for a toddy as if I had just awoken in the aftermath of an avalanche, in a blanket of snow—I would never learn the outcome of my hero's lust for love or for revenge.

I set down my glass with a thud—this also observed by the inn-keeper with a marked lack of appreciation—and, as if to exonerate my action by pointing out that his table remained undamaged, I pulled the sheaf of papers from it and waved them in the air. The glass, miraculously escaping a plunge to the floor, I rescued with my right hand and lifted to my lips. And it was thus—for I admit I had had no further interest in the contents of the bundle of papers recently confided to my keeping, now Heathcliff's line had been drawn across the page—it was with my left hand that I brought the smudged and crumpled pages up to my eyes. *ISABELLA'S STORY*, ran the legend across the top of one of these unappealing sheets, in a hand both large and, while attempting to be plain, difficult to decipher. No author was attached to this title, though I fancied I smelled violets, or roses, like the dried petals collected by my mother in a bowl, in my far-off home in Leeds.

I decided to read—if only to discover more of the man I now wished above all to emulate. Indeed, I saw his name there soon enough. But whether this new and unknown writer put down the truth was impossible to ascertain.

EDITOR'S NOTE

We are bound to declare, with the discovery of the following pages, our total ignorance of their provenance. Were they written by a schoolgirl so infatuated with the character of Heathcliff that she could not prevent herself from imagining the unimaginable: that is, the life of a bride of this Romantic anti-hero? Is this the final, true cry of woman wailing for her demon lover?

We cannot say, but assume the pages to have been secreted in the antique shop where the 'Newby manuscript' came to light and pushed in with it by a member of the Braithwaite family, proprietors of the shop for over two hundred years. What is irrefutable is that Isabella Linton, sister of Edgar and thus sister-in-law of the ill-fated Cathy, did marry Heathcliff in Wuthering Heights, *and repented her elopement exceedingly. She ran away to live in the south and was the mother of young Linton Heathcliff.*

CHAPTER ELEVEN

ISABELLA'S STORY

He came one evening when the sun was going down over Gimmerton chapel, earlier than I liked to see it doing for I had come to hate autumn and the apples that reddened in the orchard where I was sent to pick fruit for supper at The Grange. It was September, and he had been away three years—or so he told me on the second day we met there, under trees heavy with plum and crab apple and quince. On the first day, I saw only a man I had always heard called the Gypsy up at The Heights—and yet saw him now as if we had never met before.

It is hard to describe the effect the stranger Heathcliff had on all who encountered him in those last months of 1783. Some, like Nelly Dean, said money was what made the difference in the rough stable lad who had left The Heights and ran away one night as if he never intended to return. After all, there had been nothing to look forward to in the house where Hindley Earnshaw drank away the few profits from the farm. Why had Heathcliff come back there when there was so little to gain by it? people asked. To flaunt his wealth, came the reply, from those who liked to make out they knew best. But soon I knew better still: Heathcliff came back a rich man in order to kill those who had slighted him; and by marrying Catherine Earnshaw, my brother had offended most of all.

I am Isabella Linton and I grew up at Thrushcross Grange with my brother Edgar. I was eighteen years old when I ran off to get married, and my brother never spoke to me again. Then I ran from my marriage, also—there is a lot of running in this story—and I went south to live, far from the moors that rise above us at home, threatening us like a horizon where a storm gathers, ready to break even when it is a fine day. My story becomes obscure at this point and Nelly Dean—dear Nelly, the housekeeper who cared for the monster my brother married and did nothing from that day but scold and upbraid me for the slightest thing—'Isabella, don't snivel like a child!'—'Isabella, if I catch you speaking with that man again I shall go directly to Mr Linton'—said to anyone who cared to ask after me that I was dead. She visited us once at The Heights (and by 'us', which sounds so much like a happily married couple I have to confess I describe the very opposite, myself and the devil, Mr Heathcliff). She had not good to report of my swollen eye—and worse, of my legs, blue from the fiend's kicking when I was thrust down on the ground and had no strength to get away from him. I daresay she went straight back to The Grange and my dear brother decreed that I was no longer to be visited, I could not be a part of the polite society we had enjoyed in the past. I had pined to remove myself from the constrictions, as I then saw them, of the life my brother led, the life our mother and father had before him: fine linen, meals that chimed with the fancy clocks all hung with crystals that rung in breakfast, luncheon and a sumptuous evening meal, maids in starched aprons who came silent-footed to answer every summons. I yearned—foolish child that I was—for the honesty of a life out in the open, such as I had seen my sister-in-law, a child of the moors, lead in her young days at

The Heights. I was jealous of Cathy already, I suppose: she captured Edgar so completely. And he had been my friend and my supporter, defending me against the ill temper of a governess or the envy of girls from good families who lived round and came to visit, for they soon saw that I was prettier than they and liked to make sly remarks and pinch me when no one saw.

So you could say my life changed from the time Edgar married Miss Earnshaw from The Heights. Whether she loved him in return it would be hard to say; and I believe Edgar was blinded by his own emotions; but once or twice, not a few weeks after the wedding, I saw the incomparable Miss Catherine—or Mrs Edgar Linton, with all the graces and favours such a position grants the possessor of the title—yawn openly as dear Edgar described his day, shooting or visiting an outlying farm. I suspected, in short, that my sister-in-law had married in haste and now observed herself to be the unfortunate owner of as much leisure as Satan could provide for idle hands, and repented her marriage. Why it was that she had come down to settle in the crimson walls and fine white satin cushions of The Grange never occurred to me; I was occupied, I suppose, in repelling the suitable young men invited to balls and dinners with the sole purpose of meeting Miss Isabella Linton of Thrushcross Grange. For it soon became abundantly clear that Catherine wished to rid herself—and my brother also, naturally—of my company at the earliest possible opportunity.

It was at the most ambitiously laid-out entertainment in my honour that I found my life changed a second time; and, fool that I was, I believed the change to emanate from Heaven and not from Hell.

It was a fine evening, September it was true, but as warm and pleasant as a summer's night. The garden, famed in the neighbourhood for its rare shrubs and highly coloured blooms, was lit with a forest of lanterns, each illumining the finely cut lawn or raised flowerbed dictated by MacGregor, our gardener. My brother had thought of everything; even Cathy had bestirred herself to throw rose petals in the great bowl of punch the butler brought in at the appointed hour; and, shy at first but soon emboldened by the fine welcome accorded him in look and speech, the swain of the moment stood by the side of the parquet floor, awaiting his partner to open the festivities with a dance.

The awaited partner, I regret to confess, was of course myself. How satisfied and smug, with children at my knee and a life without fretfulness, my life might now be, had I accepted the proposal of marriage Mr Rutherford brought with him that evening! How well provided for and comfortable, with visits to my dear Edgar every other week (the Rutherfords being no more than six or seven miles distant from The Grange). Yet—as if I had no choice but to run from all the assurances and delights of an excellent match, I rose like one walking while asleep and went from my window-seat at the end of the long drawing-room where guests thronged and music had already started to play for the dance. I walked out from the French windows into the dark and brightly-shining garden, and there I saw the man whose features, glimpsed dimly a moment or so before through glass, I both recognised and yet did not know.

And when I reached a pool of light under a lantern by the big rowan tree, I stretched out my hand and the stranger, neither bowing, taking my fingers politely in his, nor acknowledging my status as the young lady of the house, came forward and seized me by the waist instead.

We were under the tree; and the red rowan berries and feathery leaves swept across my cheeks as he kissed me. I tasted wine—and something more intoxicating still —in that long kiss. It was the taste of savage freedom—

or so I thought then, as he held me close and Edgar, concerned that the dancing could not commence without
me, came stumbling out into a pool of darkness.

'Isabella?'—but when I broke away at the sound of
my name, the stranger left me and was nowhere to be
seen.

Yet I knew, the next day, as if the words had been
whispered to me as we kissed, that I must go to the orchard, and I would find him there. As you may imagine,
I remember nothing more of the ball, the compliments of
the neighbours, or of Mr Rutherford.

From that day I thought and dreamed of no one
and nothing but the dark stranger who had come into
the closed, calm world of Thrushcross Grange like a
hurricane or—as I was to feel later when the sway he had
over me had revealed itself as inescapable, horrible in its
power—a figure from the pack of Tarot cards the old
fortune-teller kept always with her, in the cottage down
past the trees at Gimmerton crossroads. First she showed
me the hangman, old Mrs Cox whom I had known only
as an apple-cheeked ancient; hoping to please my brother's new wife (though, as I was to discover much later,
she and Miss Cathy, as the wild, wicked girl was known,
had had plenty of business together. They called up the
black arts between them, and the card of Death was surely waiting for one of us; for Cathy or for me.)

'You will go to a lake in the north where the swan
floats over his shadow,' Mrs Cox said, and she pulled a
picture from the greasy pile on the little table in her front
parlour. 'But you will find only a dream there and will
come to understand that you are never to know love—'
and she cackled, pulling out now a hideous playing-card,
not a Tarot at all, that depicted a Queen of Hearts with
corsets unlaced and breasts thrust forward into the frame.
'And your two feet will lead you from his evil ways', Mrs
Cox finished, with another peal of the laughter I had

never heard from the quiet, respectable old woman before.

With such nonsense I passed my time after that first meeting with the man Nelly Dean excoriated—but often with a tinge of affection in her voice, as I was quick to notice. 'Heathcliff will never alter his ways', she said and sighed; and I could see from her shrewd glance at me that she knew we had kissed in the orchard, a longer, harder kiss than the night before, under the rowan tree. 'He came to us that way when he was five years old. I used to tell him, "You're the son of an Indian princess and the Emperor of China" when Master Hindley had given him a good hiding and brought him low. "You can do what you will in life, Heathcliff, never forget." And he did—for isn't he a wealthier man now than Mr Edgar, even—and what he lacks in land he'll make up for in some dastardly way or another.' And here Nelly would stop herself from going on, and warn me sternly against seeing the dark stranger again. None of which, naturally, had the slightest effect on me.

For we were like two animals in heat, my sister-in-law Cathy and I, though it is painful even now to confess it. After that first evening, when the band playing in the crimson and white room and the red berries of the rowan tree lit up by lanterns, had become exaggerated, a memory of impossible romance and reciprocated passion, Heathcliff stayed away from The Grange and it was as if he had never come at all. The maids, who had been as much taken as their mistresses by the arrogant look of the stranger, pretended they had information from Leah at The Heights that Mr Heathcliff had settled in there after his long journey back from the New World. He had visited The Grange to pay his respects to Mr and Mrs Linton (and here the odd part is that the servants guessed nothing of my sister-in-law's feelings for the vagrant millionaire, imagining that I, single as I was, could be the only maid to have fallen lock, stock and barrel for our newly sophisticated neighbour). The next visit must be paid by us, as custom went, to the rough and rude house on the moors which I had known so little and despised so thoroughly, in my earlier years. Two of the maids vied to accompany Mrs Linton, when the time came to return the call. But days passed and there was no mention of an excursion. Ah, I should have understood then that the plan was not ready yet: all must be in place before it could be accomplished; and I was no more than a small —but vital—part of that all-important design.

Edgar also noticed nothing strange in his wife, and this I found most astonishing of all. Impatient with him one minute and overly-demonstrative the next, Cathy would descend the stairs into our elegant hall like a woman of loose morals, skirt bundled over her arm and breasts peeping indecorously from her dress, a parody of the dreadful playing-card Mrs Cox had frightened me with in her cottage by Gimmerton crossroads. Without any idea that I watched her—for I followed her every movement, in fear she would slip away to the stables and saddle up the pony Edgar had given her for her birthday and be off up across the heather to The Heights, rain or shine—without acknowledging my right (for was I not at the age of betrothal and she a married woman?) to fall in love where and when I pleased, Cathy nevertheless gave every indication of her own passion and had no shame in showing it. 'Edgar, my sweet' she would purr at my poor brother, who was as besotted as a mooncalf and twice as clumsy and maladroit in her presence as any brute would be, 'fetch me my shawl and we'll go out walking in the garden'. And she would rub herself up against him, this while Nelly was standing there and I was in the rocking-chair in the morning-room, all of us on a calm, grey day trying not to observe the excited antics of the mistress of Thrushcross Grange. 'Or shall we go as far as the orchard?' And I knew then that I had in turn been watched and followed; and that my kiss had been like a knife plunging right into that pretty breast. But Edgar perceived only the flesh, and almost moaned aloud at his wife's teasing. 'No, it's raining!' Cathy went on, and I knew she saw how monstrously dull the orchard would be without Heathcliff, even if her last visit there had meant seeing him kiss me. 'I'll sit here and write my letters'. And this coy harridan settled herself in the inglenook of the old fireplace while Nelly was sent for her writing-case and the rest. 'Why did not Mr Rutherford agree to visit next week with his parents?' Cathy wanted to know next; though her pout and simper showed she knew perfectly well that tales of my escapade on the night of the ball must have reached the young man's ears and quenched his desires most efficiently. 'We do not wish to offend the county, do we Edgar dear? I shall invite them once more, making clear the company will consist solely of Mr and Mrs Edgar Linton.'

These insults and insinuations were too much for me, and I left the room with burning cheeks. My resolve was heightened, however: if I had lost the respect of the neighbourhood, as my sister-in-law was anxious to make out, then I should visit The Heights without any further dilly-dallying. I—and my family later—must take the consequences.

So, by the time I set out, I was half-swooning with the need to see the man I had all my young life despised and ignored—'the Gypsy up at The Heights'. As it turned out, I did not have to travel that far to find him— but, as my flushed face and faltering step must have betrayed—I had no notion when I left The Grange in a light rain and found him no more than a mile down the road leading to the moor, whether he lingered there in the hope of finding *her* . . . or me.

I was soon to discover where I stood—if, alas, that can even be said to be the word, for I was to fall often at his cruel blows or lie prone, too numb with grief to speak, after one of his dreadful sallies. 'You'll take me to Miss Catherine', was his command, when I had sidled up to him, no more capable of showing pride or dignity in my position as sister of the master of Thrushcross Grange than my own pet dog, Fanny. 'And make no excuses about it', he added, this time with a leer I was foolish enough to believe at first was a smile. And he held up his hand with outstretched index finger, to show me what I already had a sad suspicion of: that Edgar departed for a visit of some hours to the tenants on out-lying farms, and so the house and its mistress would be able to receive the vagabond.

Heathcliff had no desire to wait while I dithered there in the lane, as I fast discovered. No sooner did the figure of my brother and his horse Paddy begin to grow smaller—and then disappear in the bend in the road that leads down to the soft landscape of our pasturage, than my companion—the very man who had kissed me a few days before in the orchard of The Grange, proceeded to do so again. Which of us indeed, did he yearn after?—but I was a fool, and knew it—for the kiss was to act as a key or open sesame to Catherine's boudoir, and no more; and before I knew fully what I did, I led him straight in there, nodding at the servants as I went to assure them that all was well.

So it was that I engineered the meeting of the man who would shortly declare his passionate intention to carry me off and wed me, with the woman he had a burn-ing aim to make love to and be with all his days, in a true union of heart and mind.

I—who loved my brother more than any man I had yet had the chance to know—betrayed him then. He did not forgive me; and it was for this, as I am in my heart

aware, that I was never again to be permitted to come
into my own home, a place I had not left in all my
eighteen years on earth. Edgar would come to know me
as one who would sell her own flesh and blood for a
touch of the Gypsy's hand or a spark from his black eyes.
It was little wonder that I was abandoned to repent my
folly with only poor Nelly to write to, or receive a timor-
ous visit from, when once I had been banished from my
childhood abode. I did not deserve my brother's love—
nor that of any decent member of society, once I had
been depraved by the returning stranger. I was ostra-
cised; and yet, when the chance came to witness the
murder of the man who had exiled me from the company of my peers, my friends and my relatives, I leapt in
to save the rogue's worthless life, so abject was my sur-
render to Heathcliff.

I skirt the subject that cannot be spoken of here; and
yet, if I am to reveal at last the terrible truth of that September evening in my brother's absence, I must for the
first and only time give account of that depravity and its
occasioning. That Hannah and Joel, two servants carry-
ing logs to Miss Cathy's boudoir (I cannot refer to her as
Mrs Linton, here: she is Cathy, Heathcliff's Cathy, and I
was blind not to see him tie her to him as closely as a
master to a slave, on the very first night of his walking
into the ball at The Grange)—that Joel, at least, may
have seen, as I was forced to do, what took place there, is
scarcely to be doubted. Whether this faithful retainer,
shocked beyond utterance by what he witnessed, then
found speech enough to report it to my brother, I do not
know. But I suspect, from Nelly's cautious silence on the
subject, that he did; and thus, as far as my relations with
family are concerned, my banishment was forever sealed.

Catherine sat at the dressing-table in her room, looking dreamily out at the garden and the hills beyond.

What came next is neither dream nor true remembering: it was as though my soul left my body in one quick flight, and as if my movements were not my own but those of an abandoned ship, sailing rudderless across a foreign sea. I could neither accord nor resist: I knew myself dead but horribly alive; and I found myself powerless to resist commands from the devil who now possessed me.

'Go there, Isabella', said Heathcliff at last, when I had stood for what seemed a century on the threshold of the once-familiar room. 'Go—and keep your tongue from wagging, or you'll know the voice this one speaks' —and here a black leather belt, studded with gold, was brandished and a sneer, transforming the newly costumed gentleman into a brute, spread across his features. 'Whatever you may see, you will inform no one', were Heathcliff's last words, as he propelled me towards a tall press that stood, as it had since my earliest days at The Grange, by the door that led onto the stairs and landing. And before I could fully accept, with a dreadful cold certainty, the absence of my true self at the inner core of my being, I was marched into the depths of the cupboard and left there, with only the keyhole for source of light and window onto my new master's activities.

At first I thought myself a child again, hiding in the silk gowns my mother kept in the press—and which remained there long after her death, for my poor father did not have the heart to move them. Then, attempting to gain a balance in my prison—and this it was, for I could no more dare to move outside and confront my captor than to hang myself with a tassel from one of the garments dangling above my head—I saw I was indeed among the dresses of my sister-in-law, or Madam, as Edgar would have had Heathcliff address her in past days. I shrank from the unintentional caress of muslin, satin or the pleated silk she'd worn on the evening of our ball at

The Grange; and as I did so, I half-fell against the door of the press, which yielded an inch or two into the room. But I went unheard; the owner of the fine dresses, visible now, could not have spied me even if a creaking door had alerted her to the presence of a stranger; and only modesty and a fear of detection by *him*, prevented me from bursting out and running from the house altogether.

Cathy lay on her back on the four-poster bed, her petticoats billowing out around her. Her face—thought pretty by Nelly, I know, but a face that could appear wild and cruel and so had long been unappealing to me—could just be seen, deep in the welter of cushions and pillows she liked to keep her company on the bed. Her cheeks were flushed—that I did see—and her hair as messed as if the moor wind had blown it out forever from the constraints of curlers and fine coiffure. A look of joy in her eyes—I had never seen them like that before, dark one moment and blue as a summer sky the next. And she wept—*she* could make any sound she wished, it was soon clear. Heathcliff, naked and brown-skinned as a child that has bathed in rock pools and lain in heather to dry —lay astride her. I thought at first—in my innocence— that they played a game together, aping their childhood days just as the sudden confinement in my mother's press had momentarily returned me to mine. But *their* childhood had indeed been different to those of the children of The Grange, if this was the case; for soon I could be left in no doubt as to the passion and reality of their lovemaking.

Afternoon turned to dusk, as it does in autumn in the North, more quickly than could be expected; and I heard Edgar's voice outside, as he dismounted from his mare and came into the hall. What were we all to do now? Would I be discovered as an accomplice to the adulterous crime? I pushed open the cupboard door; my will returned to me in a great burst; I fled.

CHAPTER TWELVE

ISABELLA'S STORY

From that time, I became a servant of the Devil—for there is no other way to describe the man I loved and hated and married, while knowing his own heart was frozen in a raging Hell. I was at Heathcliff's beck and call, aware of his undying devotion to another; and I wished a hundred times that my brother had come more quickly up the stairs on that fateful September day, to discover and arrest the sinners and expel them from our lives and home. But, as ever in our tranquil existence at The Grange, Edgar suspected nothing. I went to Nelly and complained of a headache, once I felt safe to crawl from my hiding-place beneath the stairs; and for all I know, Cathy and her devoted husband dined amicably enough together while I was put to bed by the old servant. At least there was no sound of disagreement in the house that night. The Grange was calm, and the recent visitor—or interloper, as Heathcliff certainly was—had vanished as surely as the last glow of the September day.

It took three months more of this dreadful year for me to find myself a bride and banished forever from the home I had since infancy cherished and adored. All the autumn, Heathcliff called when my brother was abroad —he had, it seemed, powers of some kind which informed him of the absence of the proprietor of The Grange and Cathy, aware also for some reason of the suitability of the time, was ever prepared for his coming—and I would see them steal off into the orchard, or even run as far as the moor, returning spangled with the muddy rain and bracken shoots where they had lain. I was not taken on these lovers' journeys—and for this I was glad; but I was not left to my own devices, either, Heathcliff ensuring I knew the occasion of their setting off and their return. He would take me aside for a passionate, stolen kiss when a tryst was about to occur, and on one occasion had me half-naked in an upper room while Cathy sought him everywhere—but however much I begged him to stay with me, he would be gone before I could plead with him any further. He used me as kindling for the flames which followed between the wicked adulterers; and I, in despair, burned as they pursued their love. It was little wonder, I suppose, that I thought it the happiest day of my life when Heathcliff took me, one January evening, to the blacksmith's forge in Scotland and had us married there. I was fool enough to believe he found himself in love with me—I suffered then and still, to think of my folly then, I suffer now. But it was only in the two months we spent together after the marriage at the blacksmith's forge that I began to learn of the diabolical tricks my new husband was able to conjure from the depths—and entertain himself by tormenting me.

We left Thrushcross Grange only just in time, as I soon came to think, for there had been fights of a very injurious nature between my brother and Heathcliff, and the former had tried on several occasions to eject the unwelcome visitor from the house. Heathcliff had been too well-instructed in the administering of bodily harm, it was clear, for poor Edgar to take him on, on his own, and footmen and workers on the estate were brought in to subdue the glass-breaking, kicking and punching miscreant who attempted to destroy the peace of our beloved home. But Heathcliff was always stronger than all of them —Cathy would cry piteously that he must go unmolested, while Edgar hesitated at her pleas—and time and again the ruffian was winner in these uneven bouts of violence.

It is painful for me to relate here the progress of the wedding journey taken by the newly married couple— that is, Heathcliff and myself—though I can hardly bear to this day the pain of describing us as such.

We were at Gretna Green, on a dark, tempestuous evening in midwinter, after our gallop north from Thrushcross Grange; we spoke our words just as so many young folk had done, who were too much in love to await the sanction of their parents or the assurance of an heiress's fortune. Yet, for us, there was to be no happy exchange of kisses, no blissful union in the rough sleeping quarters of the ancient inn. 'Well, my dear Miss Linton', was all my new spouse would say as we went to the tavern, where he would drink himself insensible before the hour was out, and a long night of blackness and desolation faced me on my wedding night, 'you are Mrs Heathcliff now . . . you must obey my wishes to an even greater degree than before. When I signal to you, go up to bed. Lie on the right side, so you heart is open to the visitations of the dead. Walk where you are led—you have my assurances that you *will* indeed return to the land of the living. Though' —and this he added with a terrible, melancholy laugh that had the other frequenters of the inn looking over at him in sudden fear and perplexity, 'you may wish you had remained in the Isle of the Damned a while longer, once you find yourself back at home with me.'

I did as I was told. Already, as I was to conclude much later, Heathcliff poisoned me with his strange potions and weeds, these smuggled in the glass of punch the hostelry offered as sly felicitation on our marriage night. Already, by the time I was instructed to mount the

stairs—by a groom now grown drunk and morbid, his
swarthy features arousing both curiosity and hostility
amongst the dour revellers of the Scottish establishment
—I knew my heart and mind to be affected, most dis-
agreeably, by the beverage. My legs trembled, but obeyed
my will—yet whose will this was, I could not say. Nor,
when I had lain down obediently on the right side of the
ill-made wooden bed, could I recognise the dreams which
came abruptly and insistently to my sleeping brain. These
were visions of great strength and clarity—but they were
not mine. I knew myself, yet could not alter or resist this
state in which I knew myself inhabited by another, one
who must now be dead.

At first, I confess to having been bewitched by the
beauty of all I saw. A sky of a deep and piercing blue hung
above the cliffs, sandy shores and emerald forests of an
island lapped by a calm and wave-crested sea. Women
with bundles on their heads walked in a market where
bright fruit was piled; long boats with carved prows bob-
bed in a harbour fronted by pretty houses, these painted
in luscious colours like the cottons and striped garments
of the thronging crowds. Wild birds, flame-red in their
plumage, raucous in their long, demanding calls, flew
down from the pinnacles of two mountains by the sea,
these so tall, like needles—yet formed of rock and bright
scrub and soaring up into the heavens. Over all was the
sound of singing, market bargaining and the cries of children; yet there was no sense of harmony here, nor of peace-
ful co-habitation: many bore, I saw, marks of wounds inflicted lately, in the form of scars across the face or on a
back bared to the sun; others lacked features or limbs
altogether, as if these had been eaten away by termites or
chopped off randomly, to leave the sufferer mutilated but
walking still. Despite the sounds I have described, no one
spoke, or looked me in the eye—it was as if, as I was to
realise with a dreadful sense of chill, the happy bustling

trading calls and clamour of the young all came from another world, a world I could no longer enter. I walked alone, amongst the dead.

I cannot say how many times I woke—or tried to wake—from the nightmare, on that long, dark winter night in the Border inn. I know only that the face of Heathcliff, wearing the sardonic, devilish expression I had believed myself enamoured of, in the safety of my brother's home, appeared again and again amongst the people of this distant, sad and high-coloured place. His eyes looked out at me from under the brows of men and women manifesting the imprint of chains or the deep marks of whiplash, on their flesh; and his angry, insolent smile took in the quay, the prison and the market-place with the same force of contempt and superiority I had admired and craved at home. But now, seeing him thus —surrounded by his people and gloating at the gold that made him apart from them, master instead of slave—I feared him and I prayed for release from his dreadful powers.

You will know by now that I did not find freedom —for a time, at least. If Heathcliff came up to bed on our wedding night, the drug he had administered did not wake me or let me know it: I lived in that far port, with all its cripples and its dead memories of a happy life, until a frosty morning showed at the window-pane. When the sun rose, we rode north of the border; and here, among the burns that widen as they come down the hillsides, to open out into a great loch, I believe the man—or demon—I had married, searched for a lost memory of his own. It was cold, but we climbed, in heather and cloudberries, to the summit of a mountain where a cairn marked the highest point. Here, Heathcliff gazed down at the land and the expanse of black water below. He seemed to identify a field where a shepherd walked with his dog across the grass. But nothing was said to me, other than to give orders—and soon we moved on.

For all that, I had the distinct sensation in those days by the still, dark stretch of deep water—and in the whitewashed inn where we stayed, cold in the fireless room but never warm in each other's arms—that another intelligence from my husband's dictated our trajectory and took charge of our lives. Heathcliff was ever brooding, starting up suddenly when a chance cruelty or opportunity for malice came his way; but sometimes, as if in despair, he would run along the dark roads or tracks we tramped each day, these bordered by larch or tall pines and seeming to constrict us further as we went. Someone or something kept this strange, half-human being as obedient to their will as his own dreadful spells and savage gods had rendered me to him. He acted as he was bid; and the worst of it lay in the nature of the charm the poor brute was subject to: an undying love for the wife of another.

I tried at first to cure him of his obsession with her. 'Cathy', I heard Heathcliff cry in his sleep; or at times when he wandered beneath the ruined walls of Castle Douglas, where he sought her. 'Cathy, come back to me', he begged, by the banks of the brown River Yarrow that runs down there through snow—'Cathy' he would sob, as if the word was written in the stones and ditches of that blank landscape. Then he would return to my side and march on. He belonged there—he had been placed there, so it seemed to me, by an imagination that burned to enslave him forever in a Border song of anguish, betrayal, death. I had no place there; but for a while, for I could neither stay nor leave, I accompanied him through the frozen Hell where he was condemned to remain until death freed him to rejoin his love.

'Tell me, Isabella'—we sat one night at a table in the modest inn at Tibbie Shiels, on the northern shore of St Mary's Loch—'tell me, do you believe in happiness? Do you cling to the hope, my poor child, that you will find it in your marriage—that I will sigh for you one day, as I do for my love, the light of my life, at present? Do you imagine, if *she* should die—' and here Heathcliff looked across at me, his black eyes alight with the contempt I had come to expect from him, 'do you live in hope, Isabella, that I would shift my affections to my darling bride?' And he sat back in his chair and laughed, his face caught between the shadows of the falling night outside, and the glow of flames from the fire that leapt in the grate behind him. 'You are of the opinion that your sop of a brother, Edgar, would grieve more deeply than I, at the loss of Catherine', he said, and his voice was low now, for the first time since we had run away together, on that night which was to mark the ending of a life both indulged and happy: my life with the brother so regularly condemned by my husband that I could no longer hear the hurtful words.

'Why do you imagine that others cannot suffer as you do', I replied—in part, I suppose, because I had been addressed in this unusual, thoughtful tone—and also by reason of sheer habit, for I knew myself to be little better, in these new days, than an automaton.

'You, who were once of a keen disposition, my Isabella', said Heathcliff, and as so often before he took my sad thoughts straight from my mind. 'It amazes me that you should sink to little more than a serving-girl in your intelligence and ambition in life.' And the monster gave a loathsome bellow of laughter which brought tears welling once again from my eyes. 'Can you not understand that *no one*'—and here he thumped the table where we sat in the low-ceilinged, smoky little room of the lochside inn, so that the cat, a tabby with a markedly ferocious expression, was forced into flight—'no one suffers as I do, my dear wife. There is a special antechamber in Hell reserved for me, Mrs Heathcliff—and the difference lies in the fact that I inhabit it already, whereas the other poor sinners in this dreadful world live only in anticipation of the comforts provided there'. This time, no laughter accompanied the desperate testimony; and my much-regretted spouse fell into a long silence. Rain began to fall, it covered the pines and firs that fringe the loch in a silvery blur; and soon I could no longer feel where the misery invading me ended and the weeping skies of the outside world began. There was no hope, for me or for Heathcliff—I believe I saw this truly then; but it may also indicate a measure of the extent to which I was bound to this uncanny being, that I should place us together still, in dreams and my imaginings.

After a few days more we left the Ettrick Forest, the dark waters of St Mary's Loch and the bleak valley of the Yarrow, where this half-man, half-devil seemed drawn as if by a will stronger than his own. When we walked there, on sliding snow beside the frozen brown burns, he was at his mildest—if that is the term—and I would think that one day, if we became accustomed to each other, Heathcliff would learn to like my company, at least, even if he could never love me while Cathy lived. But the yearning, quizzical expression he directed to the tops of the larches —or the small smiles he sometimes lavished on bare hills, snow drifts and distant sheep pens of crumbling stone that stood against the horizon in the fast-falling light, were for another, not even Cathy, I believe; and certainly not for me. Someone or something knew the inner workings of his soul; he obeyed their commands and he could no more escape from them than could I from him.

Chapter Twelve

I did escape, however. You know the story of our time at The Heights, when we returned from two months in a country that soon became as vivid and unbelievable in my mind as the bright-coloured land of my dreams, the land of the maimed and dead across a far sea. You have heard tales of violence in that accursed place, where the master, the drunken Hindley Earnshaw, fell each day and night deeper and deeper into Heathcliff's power, his passion for gaming earning a mountain of debt which the wretched child Hareton, Hindley's child from an earlier, more promising time, will never have the ability to repay. The violence arose from this terrible situation; and I, who had become slothful and slatternly, surly in my hatred of the brute I was chained to in that remote and hideous place, longed only for the two men to fight it out and for Heathcliff to die.

Cathy it was who died as her child was born, a puny seven months baby, just as the first lambs appeared in the Gimmerton fields. I heard of it from Nelly Dean: she loved the infant from the start; but Heathcliff's terrible grief, combined with my own no less appalling suspicion that my brother Edgar might not be the father of the child, numbed my heart almost to the point of extinction. How should I reply to my brother, if he should himself suspect the paternity of the child? My guilty knowledge of the whole affair—my participation, even, as I must see it, in their sinful acts—would show clearly on my face if he were to ask me.

As with so many instances of fear and dread, this did not occur; but worse did. On the night of what appeared to me at the time to be the last and fatal battle between Hindley and Heathcliff—he who passed his days and nights in the graveyard now, with little more than a black eye to give to his wife on the few occasions we came together in the hall or kitchen of The Heights—I found my courage and I walked out into the night.

Whether the brute had grown so enmeshed in his death-worship of Cathy that he had clean forgotten to administer the drugs to keep me a zombie—as I learned later I had surely been, a woman possessed of a dead woman's self—I do not know. But on the night of that great fight, when a knife, directed at my throat, had only narrowly missed its destination, I knew myself capable of going, and of caring little whether Heathcliff lived or died. I had saved him that night once, from Hindley's murderous rage; and I feared my allegiance, shown in my unexpected loyalty—yes, as unforeseen by myself as by him—would bring me back, a boomerang, to the source of my hatred and despair.

I am living proof that it did not. I have only one reason for the guilt I sometimes suffer, when I look back on the events which succeeded my departure from that evil place. Had I remained there, a beaten wife, a sad relic of the pretty, spirited girl I once had been, I could have saved poor Hindley from his untimely death. For six months after the death of Cathy, her poor drunken brother died, too: and here is a matter for grave suspicion, once again. Hindley Earnshaw was found dead by none other than Heathcliff, at the end of a night's heavy drinking; and I have to declare that Mr Kenneth the apothecary, with whom I kept up a correspondence for some years after settling in the South, near London, expressed his own doubts as to the causes of the death. Nelly, who also wrote to me, gave her assurances that old Joseph the servant had considered Master Hindley to be in perfectly good—if inebriated—health, a short time before he was sent to fetch Mr Kenneth. Did Heathcliff murder Hindley Earnshaw? In my own opinion, and as principal witness of the terrible enmity between the two men—he did.

Chapter Twelve

My dreams for a long time after leaving The Heights contained the most inescapable and horrible visions of the man I married—or rather, the man who married *me* purely from motives of revenge. He had lost Cathy; now, since her brother Hindley's death, he is master of Wuthering Heights, every inch of which was mortgaged to him by the wretched Hindley. I dream of the window in the kitchen there, smashed by his fist; then of the knife that whistled past my cheek in its dreadful trajectory. And I see the devil in my nightmares again, the devil who is Heathcliff, when he steals in late at night when I am long gone, and smothers the snoring Hindley with a pillow until he is dead.

CHAPTER THIRTEEN

THE DEPOSITION OF HENRY NEWBY

I write this in haste in the snug of the Black Bull. There is no more to Isabella's story, save the following lines on a separate sheet:

ೞ

'I went to see Nelly Dean and she was most displeased with me, though kind in the end as she can be counted on to be. Oh, what would I do without Nelly . . . but it is long since I have laid eyes on her now, and it saddens me greatly that my parting words should have occasioned in her a rage which I have never seen in the old nurse. "Why, Nelly", I said, when she had dried my cloak and bandaged the wound at my throat, where the knife had grazed the skin, all this preparatory to my flight south (I would board the coach where it halts at Gimmerton crossroads; my friend Lucy would take me in, I knew, to her house near London; and I had gold enough from my dear dead parents to sustain me until I was settled somewhere of my own)—"my good Ellen Dean", I went on, "I imagined you knew all along of the greatest insult a man can pay his wife, that of betraying her with another. I saw it in your eyes, I believed, when you came to The

Heights and witnessed my degradation and misery there.
You understood that Heathcliff dreamed and pined for a
woman who was not his Isabella, and indeed I was a
bride of merely a handful of weeks."

' "I saw your unhappiness", Nelly answered briefly;
but her expression was clouded, her regard full of enmity,
even suspicion: did she assume I had invented the meetings my dear husband had arranged with Catherine?—
lovers' meetings, as they were, and if she did so, what
could she think had been my motive in dragging the reputation of my poor dead sister-in-law to the level I inhabited—a place where there is neither respect nor affection from the world? Surely Nelly knew me well enough,
since I was small, to refuse to credit invention of this
kind on my part?

' "September", I said, and I coloured red at the memory of the day in Cathy's boudoir; and of my own shame-
ful inability to burst free of the cupboard there and run
forever from the dreadful scene. "Not long after the ball
Edgar gave for me—" and again I faltered, unable to
meet Nelly's eyes. "You cared for Miss Cathy long enough
when she was a child", I tried to remind the old nurse,
and thus hoped to obscure her feelings of anger towards
me. "You heard—and saw—the declarations of undying
loyalty between your young mistress and Heathcliff. So
why—Nelly, you should not be surprised to learn this
loyalty was—" But I could not introduce such a word as
consummation, when I remembered the wild love-making
I had been forced to witness in my brother's marital bed,
a scene often repeated, I have no doubt, in those autumn
months when Heathcliff wooed me, readying me for the
elopement to Gretna Green. "You must have known of
their feelings for each other", I went on. "Nelly, what can
the matter be? You must believe me, surely?"

'There was a long silence, then Nelly Dean informed me that she did not doubt my word, and that it was

best to leave the subject for ever now, as the burden of my information would make everything even worse, should my poor brother hear of it. "And why?" said Nelly, as I pestered her nonetheless for the reasons for her sorrow and anger—"You ask me why, my dear child, innocent as you still are, for all the wicked follies you have now committed by allying yourself for a lifetime with one who brings only turmoil wherever he may go. By this I mean Heathcliff", she said, with a great sigh. "It is with horror and deep regret that I hear of his approaches to your late lamented sister-in-law, Mrs Linton."

'I could prise no more from Nelly, however much I pestered her for her reasons, and so it was that I left The Grange that night with as much secrecy and despatch as when I came. I resolved to put my old life behind me, to start afresh in the South, and to think no more of my existence up until this day.

'This was harder, as you may imagine, than I could have thought. From those who have been wed to a murderer—or to one who causes a married woman to commit adultery—there will be instant understanding. But—fortunately, you may say—they are not many.

'I write this as evidence, should my life be threatened by a visitation from my past, of having met with Ellen Dean at Thrushcross Grange on 3rd May 1784. The fact I am pregnant—Heathcliff does not know of it—I did not reveal to the old nurse.'

CR

My state of mind may be imagined, on reading this last, pathetic attempt on the part of a brave young woman to rediscover her spirit, resume a life free of evil dominance and live in peace far from her tormentor. And she is with child! How can Isabella survive the cruel fate that pursues her—how can she escape this devil who is as deter-

mined, I now understand, to destroy all that may promise happiness or prosperity on this earth, as Our Lord
Jesus Christ was intent on saving us poor sinners.

How can it end? Can it be true that Heathcliff is in
fact a murderer? It seems all too true, as Isabella imag-
ines his dastardly smothering of Hindley Earnshaw as he
lay snoring and drunk at The Heights that night: should
she not see that he is reported directly to the authorities
and have him tried for murder? The man whose debts
have brought the rogue Heathcliff all the ownership of
land and buildings at Wuthering Heights, ends his life at
the hands of an interloper . . . a Gypsy brought home by
old Joseph Earnshaw from Liverpool . . . and no one asks
questions in the neighbourhood, apart from Nelly Dean,
that is, who wondered if there had been 'fair play' up on
the moors that night. Owner of an ancient name, father
of a son, Hareton, who shall never now inherit the home
that should rightly be his, Hindley Earnshaw surely de-
serves better that this ignominious death, its true circumstances kept silent by all concerned. Where is Mr Kenneth, the apothecary who attended Hindley on that occasion—and many more? Is that all they care for, the gold
the brute Heathcliff carries in his purse—is this the reason
for the disgraceful lack of an inquiry into the crime?

All these thoughts pursued me out into the snow and
drizzle. There had been a thaw followed by a savage return to freezing, the lane I had come on was now almost
invisible. In a small wood on the far side of the track, a
battalion of crows set up a jeering as I hurried by; otherwise, no sound came from the landscape, submerged as it
was in a deadly blanket of whiteness. Yet I had no desire
to go back into the inn, despite it being heated by a blaz-
ing fire, and with lamps set on tables to encourage bevvy-
ing folk to stay there a while longer. I had, I sensed, an
important mission to perform; and I walked back in the
direction from which I had come, with the intent of a

man who would save an ill-treated member of the human race from further persecution or possibly from death. For every instinct in my body told me there was no time to lose in the rescuing of Isabella Linton (as I shall name her: an innocent such as she has no reason to be chained to the name Heathcliff all her days). How I had worshipped that devil—as she had! alas!—before learning the truth of his evil sorcery! How I had prepared to lay down my own life for him, when first reading his own accounts of a wild and lonely childhood; how misled by the power of fiction and how foolish I now saw myself to have been!

I cannot give an account here of the strength and apparent reality of the feelings which seized me on that morning, after reading of Isabella's experiences with the fiend. I dismissed from my mind absolutely the fact that I had considered all Heathcliff's revelations as pure fabrication, earlier: I dreamt, in short, only of those characters who had entered, so it seemed to me, my very bloodstream, to become indefinitely more real than those I had sat with in the Black Bull or visited only yesterday in their homes. I lived—I breathed—the sad, tortured lives of Cathy, Heathcliff—and now the wretched Isabella. There was no other time or place for me, than Thrushcross Grange and The Heights. And my thirst for the next instalment was rendered more intense by the hope that I might alter its content by my own efforts: I would find the ill-treated sister of Edgar Linton and make her welfare my sole concern.

CHAPTER FOURTEEN

THE DEPOSITION OF
HENRY NEWBY

I walked on, and soon saw the outline of the modest farmhouse where the shepherd's wife had sheltered me, in
what now seemed an age ago—before I had learned of
the true nature of the man whose confessions I had found
so beguiling. I had one aim: to learn, from that good
woman, the whereabouts of the old nurse Ellen Dean—
for surely she had referred to Nelly as her grandmother?
That the keeper of the family secrets of all the Earnshaws
and Lintons might still be living—and not too far from
here—was tantalising, beyond the limits of toleration: I
hastened my step, caring little when I fell in drifts or slid
across icy puddles. The house, marooned in a pocket of
cloud as hard to see through as the snow it undoubtedly
contained, was at least its substantial, unchanging self, as
far as it was possible to ascertain; and if my emotions had
undergone a sea change since understanding the bestiality
of my one-time hero (and falling in love, I confess, with
his young bride, along the way) the simple Yorkshire farmhouse had not. Here, in the prosaic tones so comforting
to me, Mrs Cecily Woodhouse would reveal the name of
her grandmother's village (or maybe the address of Thrushcross Grange?—the very thought excited me, at the possibility that Nelly Dean might live there still, retired after

a long lifetime of service to Isabella's family). My most pressing questions would be answered: surely, Nelly knew whether the child taken in by the Earnshaws all those years ago, and considered a vagrant, a Lascar, had at the apex of his strange career, when rich from his plunder of the New World, ended up a murderer. And, as Isabella's last statement averred, there was a correspondence between nurse and former charge which would be of the greatest interest to me. What I most dreaded to hear—that Heathcliff had succeeded in discovering his wife's new dwelling-place, and even that he had removed the child from her—I would at least hear from one who knew, and no other. Nelly, seeing another Joseph Lockwood in this stranger (I had already, in my mind, imagined myself at The Grange and been admitted; even already, as if in sincere imitation of poor Mr Lockwood, in the early throes of a heavy cold). I saw myself in bed, tended by Nelly despite her advanced years, sipping grog while she recounted to me the story I now could not exist without, the tale of Heathcliff and the sad aftermath of his unholy love.

I must have slowed down considerably, once in the grip of these fancies, for I was only halfway up to the shepherd's house before I found myself overtaken and almost pushed aside into a threadbare collection of bushes —not so much a shrubbery—that grew by the door. The shoulders and back view of the man who now turned the handle roughly and walked in, were familiar to me: this was John Brown, the sexton, the very man I had followed on my journey to the Black Bull last evening; but the habitual pleasantness of his expression (for he turned once, from the narrow lobby and looked out, still not observing me, it seemed) had quite gone, to be replaced by a look of intense grief. What it was that I now stumbled into, I shall endeavour to explain.

John Brown, as he informed me in gruff tones when I had finally emerged from the fog-shrouded trees and been acknowledged as a caller to the house, was visiting the shepherd to express his condolences on the death of the latter's wife. The expiry of Mrs Woodhouse had been sudden, taking place in the early hours of this morning, when all the inhabitants of Haworth were engaged either in celebrating the coming New Year or in sleeping off their revels. News had been brought by one of the old shepherd's hands; it was too late to call at the doctor's house, and burial arrangements would have to be made as soon as possible. 'When there is a winter such as this one', said the sexton, and he guided me through into the kitchen as he spoke, 'I cannot express surprise at the loss of so many souls. Some, it must be said'—and here, standing in the cold and empty kitchen, he gave a deep sigh, placing both hands on the modest pine table and looking across at me with a questioning air, as if to wonder wordlessly how acquainted I might be with those he had committed lately to Haworth churchyard—'some, of an undoubtedly great standing in the world of letters, though this is not yet known. Possessors, it can be claimed, of the highest genius'. And he sighed again; while the slow, shuffling steps of the recently widowed shepherd could be heard on the steep stairs to the upper floor.

'But—' I began. I felt myself on the brink of a new discovery, to be unfolded by the handsome, good-hearted sexton; but I also sensed, to my shame, that I might learn nothing, with my hoped-for informant gone and all chances of finding out the truth vanishing into thin smoke before my eyes. The shame, naturally, came from that humanity I shared with the poor dead woman: that I should mourn her end simply because it removed my likelihood of finding Nelly Dean, was, I knew, reprehensible in the extreme. But—fight against it as I might, I could not overcome my exasperation—rage, almost—at missing the rest of Heathcliff's tale (ghastly though it might be) by so brief a margin. What could John Brown tell me of, that could count half so much as the continuing exploits of the children of the calm (as I had come to see the Lintons, in their downland prosperity) and the children of the storm, Heathcliff and Cathy? That I was wrong again, soon became clear to me.

The old shepherd came in, and the sexton went to commiserate with him. In low voices not audible from where I stood, by the unlit range under the window in the kitchen, funeral and burial arrangements were discussed and finalised. Then, as if the thought of the graveyard returned him again to his recent tragic tasks, John Brown strode over to me and continued as if he had not had occasion to break off.

'You are in Haworth to seek Ellis Bell', said the sexton, and I suffered, not for the first time, a sense of horror at the memory of the night I had passed at the Parsonage, and of the sleepless, dream-haunted hours in the small study over the sitting-room where old Mr Brontë would sit by the fire and prepare his sermons; and where I had found Heathcliff's tale burning merrily on the coals. 'I must inform you that Ellis Bell—Miss Emily Brontë as you are aware by now—was not the author of the novel *Wuthering Heights*. It is an error which would otherwise persist down the centuries, Mr Newby; I have permitted your entry to this house—a house of bereavement—solely in order to inform you of this; and to request that you in turn inform the publisher Newby to correct the name appended to the work.'

That John Brown had taken the time and trouble to ascertain my credentials was undeniable; that he in turn suffered from an obsession with the book now began to become uncomfortably clear. 'You will return to Leeds forthwith', John Brown said—still with the measured tones of a Yorkshireman, but always with the undercurrent of excitement I had detected as he commenced his peroration. 'You will inform your uncle Thomas Cautley Newby of the identity of the true author of this great work. All copies printed previous to these instructions shall be burned or pulped without delay.'

I was, I confess, unable for a while to reply to this peremptory demand. A collie scratched at the back door; the old shepherd fiddled at the range with a scuttle of coal and a basket of pine cones. A wintry sun, defying the white fleece settled everywhere on hill and beck, shone incuriously in the sky. Anyone might think—so I concluded miserably as we stood on together in the frosty kitchen—that John Brown and I had met for an amicable talk, to finalise, perhaps, the nature of the headstone required for poor Mrs Cecily Woodhouse. The sexton's threatening manner remained, for the time at least, virtually concealed.

'I came here to find where I may discover Nelly Dean', I blurted. There was, as I considered later, some cunning in my response: I had not failed to study my father in court; and something told me that an abrupt change of subject may unnerve an antagonistic witness and force him to tell the truth. Besides this, of course, I was more set than before, if this was possible, on talking to the good housekeeper and exacting from her the rest of Heathcliff's story, and Isabella's fate.

'Mr Newby.' To my surprise, a smile flitted across the sexton's fine features. 'You jest with me, I am sure. I like it in a man; and I must add that the true author of the pages where you have already found Nelly Dean liked nothing better than a practical joke. Branwell Brontë liked to scatter largesse for the village children, down by the bridge. He laughed at their glee—and their discomfiture at finding the pennies were sticking to their hands when they had grasped them. Branwell loved to enact the role of Alexander Percy, Earl of Northangerland—and to enter the kingdoms of Angria and Gondal. Especially Gondal', John Brown added with a pensive nod of the head.

I now felt myself to be in the presence of a madman. Coupled with this unpleasant realisation was an atmosphere in the tiny kitchen that was well nigh unbearable: the old shepherd had piled the range with all manner of larchwood and the like, and the smoke from the blaze filled the room. An unpleasant suspicion that the strong presence of rosemary and some other medicinal plant—if these they were—in the fire, were there as fumigation following the death of the shepherd's wife, brought me to a state of faintness. The sun, trying harder than before to dissolve the white mist outside, came in sharp as a needle straight into the eye, to increase my discomfort. The back door, bolted still, was just visible through the smoke. I reached it, pulled back the bolt, and received the collie, frozen by now and shaking with hunger and cold, right into my arms. John Brown pulled me back towards him, in the kitchen, and the door, a stable door which I could have tackled better if I had seen its composition, swung shut again.

John Brown guided me to a narrow, rickety chair at the side of the table and stood over me as he delivered his instructions. 'You are selected—and though this can be repeated only on pain of death, I confide it to you as a mark of my expectations of you, Mr Newby—you are chosen, as was your subject, to enter the Lodge of the Three Graces. The ceremony will take place immediately, with old Joseph and two others who are awaited here, in attendance. When you are accepted into the Order, you will be free to commence your researches into the life of Branwell Brontë. Without full knowledge of Freemasonry, the work could not be complete.'

'Freemasonry?' I echoed the sexton, whose looming person—for the fumes from the stove, in response to some new combustible, had now turned black—resembled that of a medieval devil, rising from the flames of Hell. 'My subject—?' I was aware of sounding pitiful, and no doubt doubly feeble, imprisoned as I was; but no escape seemed possible from this farmhouse at the foot of the hills outside Haworth.

'You are Branwell's biographer', the sexton said impatiently. 'The firm of Thomas Cautley Newby will publish the Life of the author of *Wuthering Heights*, in conjunction with the new edition of that great work'.

I lowered my head onto the table, like nothing so much, it occurred to me, as a real prisoner, tired after hours of cruel interrogation by the authorities. My eyes smarted and stung; tears from the vile smoke ran down my cheeks; and now a bout of coughing wracked my chest and throat. I prayed—and never had I prayed more earnestly—for release from my terrible situation.

Release came—in the shape of old Joseph himself, who fetched a glass of water, pulled open the stable door, and led me to the open air to drink. John Brown, who busied himself with a roll of richly embossed fabric—this intended, it can only be supposed, for my initiation—had his back to us as he pulled at a bag containing the regalia and proceeded to roll it out along the floor.

I saw my chance, and seized it. The bare hill, lit now by a sun that made glistening furrows in the deep snow, was reached, and a cleft in the hills afforded me a hiding-place, all within less than two minutes of running. My heart pounded, and I could barely hear the shouts of the sexton as I darted along the side of a ravine and teetered further on the edge of what appeared to be the resting-place of an avalanche.

I was free; and I had the satisfaction of knowing my efforts would not all be in vain. For, as I took my first steps into Haworth Moor, I demanded in a whisper of the shepherd where I might find Wuthering Heights—it was my last hope, I knew, of discovering the woman the shepherd's wife at the farmhouse had referred to as Nelly Dean.

Old Joseph pointed straight ahead, to Top Withens as he said. And I ran, on and upwards, still hidden by the curve of the moor from the eyes of John Brown, the sexton.

EDITOR'S NOTE

Mania, as we are advised by a close friend in the medical profession, can be triggered both by anxiety and by alcohol or drugs.

We have reason to suppose that Henry Newby's hallucinations and the 'fever' to which he refers (not to mention the extreme improbability of a packet 'from Ellen Dean' having actually been received by him) were caused by the ingestion of a substance more perilous to the health even than the reading of sensational novels. This is laudanum—which, as we know, soothed the pains and fuelled the imaginations of nineteenth-century England.

We spent some time deliberating on whether to present to the coming symposium on 'Emily and Heathcliff: an Exploration' the tragic evidence of the young lawyer's habit. In the interests of truth and honesty, we decided to go ahead.

CHAPTER FIFTEEN

Letter from Henry Newby to Thomas Cautley Newby.

February 12th 1849

Dear Uncle,

I write to offer my heartfelt apologies for the delay in replying to your many enquiries as to the whereabouts of further chapters of the novel by Ellis Bell, the retrieval of which was the reason for my being despatched to Haworth six weeks ago.

It is difficult for me to answer, Uncle, in full at least, without incurring your further wrath on the subject. You must believe, even if this means relying on the most credulous side of your nature, that the mission proved almost impossible, despite my most vigorous efforts to save Mr Bell's manuscript from destruction at the hands of (supposed) members of the family, and servants intent on obliterating the novel from existence.

I refer to the late author of those fragments I did succeed in rescuing as Mr Ellis Bell, for the good reason that I am now the possessor of important information as to the true identity of the writer of *Wuthering Heights* (and thus, surely, its successor). The pseudonym Ellis Bell did not mask the name of the youngest of the sisters of Haworth Parsonage, Miss Emily Brontë, but that of her brother,

Branwell. The source of this information must be
kept for the time, secret: but I do assure you, dear
Uncle, that I hope soon to be in a position to ac-
quaint you with the whole story surrounding these
works and their authorship. The unfortunate circumstance of my illness following New Year in Haworth
must explain my otherwise unpardonable delay in
replying to you. I can hope and trust, only, that my
nearness to death over the past six weeks, with a
fever contracted on Haworth Moor and an inflam-
mation of the lung that succeeded it, will occasion
an avuncular concern for your nephew. If I add that
doctors called in by my good father feared that I
might also be on the point of losing my sanity, I
again can only hope that this will not lead you to
lose all sympathy for me. Perhaps—though I con-
cede that my father and brothers do not consider
my confiding in you in this manner either wise or
commendable—you will understand me better if I
outline to you that fateful last day at Haworth, when
a violent snowstorm had me walking foolishly up in
search of a farmhouse, Top Withens (thought to be
the origin of Wuthering Heights: you may appreci-
ate that my efforts were all for you, and for the future prosperity of Thomas Cautley Newby, publisher), and discovering myself lost, alas, in more
ways than one.

I will not conceal the fact that those chapters I
had read on the subject of the villain Heathcliff, his
passion for Catherine Earnshaw Linton and his ab-
ominable treatment of the young Miss Linton, had
me eager to find out more. A chance encounter at a
shepherd's house by the moor led me to decide on a
stiff climb to Top Withens—that you may remark
on my evident lack of sanity in attempting this on a
day of almost unprecedentedly ferocious weather

has not failed to occur to me. Solely the knowledge that a dedicated publisher will recognise the undeniable thirst of a reader—and in this case a kinsman, employed by your distinguished firm—encourages me to hope I will not be observed by you as having entirely lost my wits. For, despite the pronouncements of doctors when once I had been taken home—and of those who found me on that dreadful moor, snow-soaked and directionless outside the ruined walls of Wuthering Heights—I was mad only in my desire to follow the characters whose trajectory you had demanded I should discover at Haworth Parsonage. Without your introduction to the barely credible world of violence, brutality and death depicted by Mr Ellis Bell, I should not have suffered the collapse both mental and physical which I have just outlined to you.

At first, on that morning just succeeding New Year—but which day it was I cannot say—I climbed easily enough up onto the moor, skirting the deep bogs and perilous precipices formed by snow and ice together. I will make no bones about the fact, Uncle, of my burning need to learn more of these unsavoury characters—and, if possible, to rescue Isabella Linton—Mrs Heathcliff, although I do not like to say the name—from any further embarrassment at the hands of her husband or any others connected to Wuthering Heights. My most pressing need was the finding of Ellen Dean—who, as you may remember from the pages published by none other than the firm of Thomas Cautley Newby, had been nurse and housekeeper at Wuthering Heights on the occasion of Heathcliff being brought from Liverpool as a boy. She had continued to serve both Lintons and Earnshaws at Thrushcross Grange, also; and, aware that Miss Isabella wished to understand the nature of the devil she had married, through untangling the mystery of his origins, I found myself honour bound to assist her in every way I could. She had settled in the South, I knew; I had every intention of writing to her in her new abode, once I had learned the truth from Nelly Dean.

Alas, all my most fervent hopes were to be dashed. I walked, or rather climbed, through the snow on the moor until the fading light and my own weakening strength almost made welcoming the idea of laying down in a bed of whiteness, without even digging down to find the heather which must lie below. A collie dog (I neglected to say the animal had followed me all the way up from the shepherd's house) urged me on, however: it clearly knew the way to Top Withens, for it began to bark long before the walls of the farmhouse appeared in the northern twilight; and while I was just capable of walking, or staggering the last hundred yards, it ran alongside me, whimpering its encouragement.

How I wish I had turned then, even if it had been a fatal enterprise, to attempt to retrace my path in the fast-encroaching darkness. How much shelter, in any case, did the ruin where I now found myself afford? I would have been better, so I was to conclude when penetrating further into a roofless building, the hall containing nothing more than a fallen mantel from the fire, the masonry strewn about over an oak floor, the flagstones cracked and filthy—I would have been better in a sheep pen with my companion the collie for company.

The moon, a half-moon that bulged like an eye over the fat cheek of the distant Stanford Moor, had risen as I made my uncertain way around the house which once had contained the passions and rages of the Earnshaws (I was certain, Uncle, that a collapsed fragment of the heraldic stone piece above the fireplace bore the initials H.E.—for the wretched Hindley and many Hindleys before him, I have no doubt, E. for the now blighted name of Earnshaw). I made my way to the window, the glass all smashed and snow piled high on the sill; and there, out by the back door, where the moor runs right up to the abandoned house, I saw them, kissing.

It was a full minute before I saw that the man, whom I had imagined to be Heathcliff, could not be he. And the young woman—how I had caught my breath at the idea I saw Isabella herself there, reconciled with her wicked hero!—was no resident of The Heights, nor of The Grange down below. She wore a dress such as my mother and sisters wore —and still do—it was very much of our day. Her lover, for so his persistent kisses proclaimed him to be, had not the height or presence of a Heathcliff: in the dim light it appeared his hair was reddish in colour, and he too wore the clothes of today, trousers and a jacket which had every appearance of attempting—and not succeeding in being—smart. They both turned; my heart leapt as I saw in my mind's eye the little sitting-room at the Parsonage where I'd passed a sleepless night; and again and again I travelled round that small room with its mezzotints and sketches hung on the walls, and saw both faces before me there.

Uncle, you know the rest. The collie dog was my helper, in the end: it brought rescue to the place where I had fallen unconscious in the ruins of Top Withens, and I was portered to safety by a team of men.

And now, Uncle, I end my letter to you. You may be interested to know that I have no further

connection with the characters I sought on that awful day, up on Haworth Moor. I know them for what
they are; and I regret my folly in chasing shadows
from the pages of a novel.

As I lay here recovering from my ordeal a few
weeks back, the post came with this strange packet
addressed to both of us. I opened it—but on seeing
that it purports to be by 'Ellen Dean' I stuck up the
envelope once more, and duly send it down to you.

Your affectionate nephew
Henry Newby

EDITOR'S NOTE

The following 'statement', purporting to be in the hand of the narrator of Emily Brontë's novel, Nelly Dean, is reluctantly included here. We own to a certain shame in presenting the clumsy efforts of a novice writer to become a published author: today, Henry Newby would be encouraged to join a Creative Writing Course at a respected university and instructed in the art of narrative. Unfortunately for us (and for his posthumous reputation) his wild surmises on the parentage of Heathcliff, etc., have come down to posterity.

CHAPTER SIXTEEN

NELLY DEAN'S STATEMENT

<u>*To Whom It May Concern*</u>

I, Ellen Dean of Thorn Cottages, Gimmerton, give here my account of the circumstances of the birth of one known as 'Heathcliff', of Wuthering Heights.

In the summer of 1764 I left my parental home east of Halifax and found my way, by way of rides in waggon-carts and by hiding in stagecoaches, to the great city of Liverpool. I was twelve years old at that time, and could find neither happiness nor acceptance in my family.

Once I was in the city I soon found myself a bed in a house purporting to be run by a woman of good family, and was foolish enough to believe her declaration that she had taken pity on one so young adrift in the world, and wished for nothing more than to give me a roof over my head until I should be old enough to fend for myself.

It soon became clear that money changed hands in this household when the other inmates, all young girls like myself, were visited by gentlemen—or by sailors or worse—as was often the case. One of the girls I befriended: she was as bewildered as I by the goings on there. She evidently had no experience, either, of our native country, for she had been a slave and was just over from the islands, though where these are or were I cannot say. She spoke a strange tongue, and became known as the Lascar maid, and some took her for the daughter of pirates.

We had not been there long when a man I had the necessary shame in recognising, came to this house of ill repute. He made it clear from the first that he came to save the fallen women and not to take advantage of them —but as he paid handsomely for the opportunity to carry out his reforms, our mistress of the house tolerated him quite happily.

This man was a cousin of my late mother, who had been an Earnshaw from Sladen Moor before she married and whose death, alas!—caused the remarriage of my father, and my own unhappy childhood.

At first I said nothing when Joseph Earnshaw came. I felt shy to be seen in these surroundings by the respectable old man, known for his hospitality at The Heights. Indeed, he would send a sheep each Christmas to my parents when my mother was alive and he wrote to her in her last illness with the kindness and affection for which he was famed throughout our county.

Joseph Earnshaw took particular trouble when trying to understand the speech of my dark-skinned friend —whom I called Sarah, for she had no name that any of us could get our tongues round when it came to calling her. Once he had ascertained that neither she nor I had yet been admitted to the cruel trade overseen by our mistress (she waited, I believe, until we were more developed as women, for Sarah was considered still too wild to fetch a good price and I, some years younger, was as thin and straight as a boy) it became Joseph Earnshaw's most devoted aim to remove us from these insalubrious surroundings. I, Ellen, as a daughter of his kinswoman, he took to The Heights where I worked as nursemaid until the death of Mrs Earnshaw, and after that as housekeeper. I was treated with the utmost consideration at The Heights by Joseph Earnshaw and Mrs Earnshaw, and for all their faults I grew to love their children, Master Hindley and his sister, Miss Catherine. But Sarah, my dark-skinned friend, could have no place with us.

On the night he came to fetch me away, my friend Sarah became very aggrieved and despondent, accusing us both of abandoning her to her fate in the brothel—for this was no more and no less than what our home was. She begged Cousin Joseph to bring her home with me, and she cried piteously when he said he could not. Sarah did not avoid her fate as a woman of easy virtue and mother of an unwanted child. I shall be haunted to the end of my days by the sight of her at the window when we left.

It was late at night when my kinsman and I set off to return to The Heights—where, despite the hour, a great fire was burning, to welcome us in.

When Heathcliff, abandoned by all with whom he came in contact, and kidnapped, so it was said, by slave traders, was found wandering in the streets of Liverpool a few years later, a local woman who once had worked in the house that had been a home to me and Sarah, saw him and wrote to the kindly old man. He came into the city and retrieved the child—his own bastard son with Sarah.

Signed
Ellen Dean
September 1801

CHAPTER SEVENTEEN

THE DEPOSITION OF HENRY NEWBY

February 28th 1849

I have a confession to make. The fault must lie with my uncle and his pressing demands for chapters from the novel left unpublished—not even submitted—at Ellis Bell's death (whoever Ellis Bell may in the end turn out to be).

I did not stick up the packet from Ellen Dean without perusing the contents: I am not cured enough yet, if such can be the term, from the reading habits formed at the time of my unfortunate visit to Haworth Parsonage. I dream at night of a woman I found in a book, who belongs more strongly in the land of the living than any maid aspiring towards marriage and motherhood in the city of Leeds. I sigh and mope over my work in the law office on occasion, still—and I must lay the responsibility for this sad state of affairs with my uncle, Thomas Cautley Newby. Had he not sent me on an errand to retrieve new tales of horror and passion conceived in the brain of a deranged author, I should be rising higher in the firm of Newby & Sons and very likely announcing my betrothal to a Miss Pontifex, whose father's engineering works abut our own offices. My mother would be delighted at the glad tidings; and a house would be surveyed and purchased on the west side of the city, with a garden where our children would play in summer.

Alas, none of this is to be. My excitement—nearly bringing on another bout of the fever suffered on Haworth Moor—has been intense since reading Nelly Dean's statement. I know more now, so I believe, than anyone else in this strange matter: I begin to know the origins of the man who is neither man nor devil. I yearn to confide my findings to the beautiful young woman who entrusted her life and future happiness to the monster; and where she seeks, I shall follow and entrust her with the secrets I have just read. Isabella shall learn of Heathcliff's early abandonment by his mother, and of his parentage. She it is who will judge Nelly Dean's silence in all those years at The Heights when Hindley Earnshaw cheated the lad of his rightful inheritance and demanded he work as a stable lad.

But who can condemn the discretion of servants? Nelly Dean knew more than she was prepared to say.

March 1st

A missive has arrived here from my uncle, expressing his disgust at the pages I sent down to him. He insists they are not by the same hand as chapters read and examined earlier: he even goes so far as to accuse me of being their author! And he asks me, in a tone both insulting and hurtful, to desist sending him this 'improbable sequel' to Mr Bell's novel.

The worst aspect of the matter lies in the nature of the material my uncle returns to me. I sit and rub my eyes in the dingy office overlooking the Pontifex works— and for the first time I wish myself securely married and settled, even if my father-in-law, with his tricks and peculiarities, might prove intolerably irksome—for what I have had returned to me by my uncle is not at all what I sent.

Ellen Dean's statement is there in the packet, it is true. But there are other pages, in an envelope of their own and addressed—he is perfectly correct in asserting that the hand bears no resemblance to that appended to earlier chapters—to Thomas Cautley Newby directly. I opened the packet an hour at least after gazing inside, and observing the signature of the writer. I am in need of air—and find myself overlooked here at Newby & Sons, by the manager of the Works, the very man who expects to walk his daughter up the aisle to wed me there.

I have walked right out of the city, and sit on a bank that has a fine view of Leeds, its smoking stacks and busy manufactories. I am as far as it is possible to be from the world outlined to me here by the lovely young woman I once had yearned for, and now find immeasurably distasteful to contemplate. I am plunged, in this landscape of dark Satanic mills, into a society far more sinful than I could have imagined possible, and completely without the morals with which the inhabitants of this great city of Leeds have been imbued since birth: I am, in short, speechless at the wickedness practised by all those who came in contact with the man who is the personification of evil, Heathcliff. This is what I read: when I have done with it, the canals and waterways of our city shall bear the pernicious testament out to sea and it will be lost forever.

CHAPTER EIGHTEEN

THE DEPOSITION OF HENRY NEWBY

The pages were in the hand of Isabella, unhappy wife of the monster, Heathcliff. At last I would learn the story of her life; and I scarcely dared, so great had my fascination with her been, to open the packet and read on. These are her words:

 CR

'I fled south from the ruin of my life, and found neither solace nor happiness in the house my friends found for me, nor relief from the pain that had been inflicted on me by the one—alas!—I still longed for and loved.

'Night and day, I dreamed of Heathcliff, and of the passion we might have had together. Each day seemed a month in duration; the season—it was May—was as uninteresting as a dull book gone through too quickly; and the fact of my secret burden, the child I carried within me, brought a pall of fear and suspicion over all I saw and all those who tried to comfort or amuse me.

'The house I had was near London and I visited a family there who entertained me very hospitably—for they had no idea, at that time, of my brother Edgar's decision to ban me from his company, or even of my imprudent marriage to the man who now maltreated the owner of The Heights, Hindley Earnshaw, forcing him into debt and drinking, and removing his property from him as he did so. I was treated as a young unmarried woman—there were rumours that I was in fact a widow and did not choose to speak of my bereavement—and admirers in plenty appeared to escort me to various amusements in the capital.

'I may say that none of this appealed to me; yet, as I pined for Heathcliff and at the same time prayed for deliverance from my unwelcome pregnancy, I began to understand that I might find the love of my life after all, and not where I had expected to seek him. For the old witch at Gimmerton had filled me with dreams and fancies—that I would come together with my own true love in Venice, the city in the sea, where the cats are fashioned from glass and good fortune follows bad like the masked dancers in the carnival.

'I became convinced of Heathcliff's undying love for me—and this I confide in full awareness of the ridicule which will accompany my statement of this belief. I waited each day for the mail-coach, as if my life and future depended on it. At night I swooned in memory of the kisses I had shared—but only as I slept—with the man who was the Devil incarnate, and yet the only one I could be with, on earth or in Hell. I would tell him of the child I carried, and he would take me in his arms, proud at last that I had brought a son into the world, for him. For I had known that a son would come from our union, and seal the love we should have consummated and perfected long ago.

'My son—for this was indeed the son I had prayed for before falling victim to my sad fancies—did not in the least resemble Heathcliff, and for this the Good Lord must be thanked. He was the image of my darling brother Edgar when he was a child, and I named him Linton.

He was my one and only reason for remaining alive, and I love him with all my heart.

'My greatest fear, at present, is that Heathcliff, father and legal guardian of young Linton, will discover us here and remove his son, who is now twelve years old. I cannot bear the idea of losing him to a godless heathen such as Heathcliff.

'But, after twelve years expiating those sins embraced so ardently in my youth, the end of my calm and contentment is in sight. I know myself to be ill; my brother, relenting at last on receiving news of my decline, comes tomorrow to bid me farewell and take my son north with him, to Thrushcross Grange. Edgar promises to guard Linton vigilantly; but I know Heathcliff and I tremble: he will be altogether too near, too near . . .'

CR

Here Isabella's story breaks off. It was dark by the time I left the sooty bank above Leeds and made my way home. I did not light the lamps when I entered my room, but lay down on my bed and lay there awake all night.

EDITOR'S NOTE

We have here attempted to show, as we conceive it, the dawning of understanding on the part of Henry Newby when confronted by the evidence regarding authorship of the 'lost' successor to Wuthering Heights. *Only an objective approach we feel can uncover the truth and reveal the genius of the much maligned Branwell Brontë.*

CHAPTER NINETEEN

HENRY NEWBY,
BIOGRAPHER

A man in his early or mid thirties—bearded, bookish, stooping—makes his way slowly up the village street of Haworth towards the Parsonage. If his progress is noted, it causes no surprise: Mr Newby, appointed biographer of the late Branwell Brontë some year or two back by his uncle, the publisher Thomas Cautley Newby, has become a frequent visitor to the home of the now-celebrated Brontë sisters. Nearly everyone with any connection to the family has been interviewed exhaustively, from the loyal Martha Brown, servant to the Reverend Patrick Brontë, to William Wood, village carpenter and nephew of Tabby, maid and nurse to Charlotte, Anne and Emily. Wood had told his story several times, this concerning the extreme slenderness of the coffin he had been commissioned to make for Miss Emily. In recording the measurements, he said he had never in all his experience made so narrow a shell for an adult: at 5 feet 7 inches by 16 inches its width would have been better suited to a child.

The reason for the delay in publication of Henry Newby's Life of Branwell Brontë, is due to the unfortunate case of libel brought against his uncle, the London publisher; and a resulting state of bankruptcy only now about to be discharged. It is a sign of the publisher's determination to continue believing in his nephew's assertions on the subject of the authorship of *Wuthering Heights*, that the volume is scheduled to go to press as soon as the final pages are completed and the manuscript sent down post-haste to Mortimer Street. The hubbub surrounding the discovery of the true identities of Currer, Acton and Ellis Bell—and the cult that has grown up around the Parsonage—(this thanks both to Ellen Nussey, a close friend of Charlotte, and Mrs Elizabeth Gaskell)—have not affected the decision to go ahead with the biography of Branwell, considered by now to be by far the least talented and interesting member of the family. Thomas, who likes to boast of a 'nose' for a good book or a commercially successful venture, is confident in his nephew's powers of detection, and his ability, doubtless inherited, to sniff out the truth in a scandalous story. Henry has passed many trying seasons in attempting to 'get behind' the romance of Branwell and his employer's wife, Mrs Robinson. He has, albeit with reluctance, passed innumerable nights in the Black Bull (he has forsworn alcohol and can be seen sipping at tea or some other beverage unlikely to have been consumed by his subject) and he has paced the graveyard countless times, observing the headstone of the young man who liked, in the fantasy life so much more appealing to him than the reality of his sad failures and drunken blundering, to see himself as Alexander Percy, Earl of Northangerland. (Henry Newby has also, naturally, been shown the tiny books written by the acclaimed sisters, these outlining the exploits of the inhabitants of the kingdoms of Angria [Charlotte's domain] and Gondal [Emily's].) The niece of old Tabby, repeating lore of past days here at Haworth, has described to the biographer the terrible sultriness of an afternoon forty years back, when the moor rose up and suffered an earthquake which nearly killed the Brontë children, Emily then being six years old and Branwell seven.

There is only one important character in the forth-coming work—a work which should 'prove', conclusive-ly, the authorship of the famous novel as being that of the maligned and neglected Branwell—and that charac-ter is the sexton John Brown, whose leonine head, against a backdrop of stormy sky, the young Brontë had painted to such effect. Brown, after a first brief meeting with the biographer (and it was possible, as Newby noted with discomfort, that, despite his beard and much-aged ap-pearance, Brown retained some memory of an earlier occasion in a shepherd's house, and his own revelation of the identity of the author of *Wuthering Heights* there) had politely declined to meet Newby further.

Today, for no reason known to this solicitor's clerk now attempting to revive the fortunes of a shady publish-ing house, Newby had been informed that John Brown will meet him at last, and at the Parsonage. It was known that old Patrick, for many years the vicar of the parish, was by now—in 1861—gravely ill and considered to be on his deathbed. Newby could only suppose that a wors-ening of the Reverend's condition had caused the change of mind in John Brown; and if the budding biographer felt a hint of petulance at the prospect of hearing from the horse's mouth (if the orifice providing the pronoun-cements of the sexton could be so termed) on the subject of the death of Branwell Brontë once again—'John! I am dying!' followed by the arrival of the Reverend Patrick, Branwell staggering to his feet, crying 'Father' and then falling dead—he made a sincere effort not to show it. That the scene might be re-enacted, for the benefit of a pious future reading public, was highly probable; certainly, Branwell's odes and ballads and pitiful scrib-blings would be brought forth, if not the sixpenny pack-ets of opium pills or fivepenny 'squibs of gin' with which he had frequently found oblivion. A reporter for the *Halifax Guardian*, a Mr Dearden, had already written to

Henry insisting that Branwell Brontë had professed himself the author of *Wuthering Heights* and that clues in the
manuscript would, when demonstrated, bring conclusive
proof of his authorship.

The coming rendezvous was not the only cause for
Newby's sense of dread. He knew, in order to satisfy his
uncle and (he hoped) restore the rocky finances obtaining in Mortimer Street, that any salacious detail apper-
taining to the sole male sibling in the Brontë family
would increase sales considerably. He had the Mrs Robinson affair off pat and had sent a précis of it to London;
and the Will 'proving' that lady's loyalty to her husband
had been despatched to Newby & Sons in Leeds, so the
fine print could properly be deciphered. Yet, apart from
tirades delivered in drunkenness at the Black Bull, and
blasphemous utterances hushed up by the devoted John
Brown, there was no real scandal to attach to Branwell,
other than the claim by this untalented nondescript that
he was responsible for his younger sister's novel. Newby
hoped, but not with a sense of coming success, that he
would dig up something buried by the sexton and (probably) by Miss Charlotte Brontë, a something that would
cause grave disapproval and also titillate the readers.

At first, the interview with the ancient Patrick Brontë
and the still-robust John Brown went much as had been
expected. The parson of Haworth, eager to spell out his
son's virtues, insisted on leading the way up to the small
room which had been shared by Branwell and his father
for many mortifying years, the impecunious situation of
the son reflected in the child's bed next to his parent,
which Branwell had had to occupy. Here, as Newby had
feared, the story of 'John I'm dying' and the respectful
staggering to his feet of the sad Branwell Brontë at the
sight of his parent, were indeed repeated, John Brown
standing just as respectfully while Patrick Brontë played
out his part. Newby had become accustomed to the rep-

etition of stories, usually described as memories, which appeared to become fixed in a kind of gelatine of unalterability each time they were brought out. He could not count the number of times he had heard of Branwell setting his bedclothes on fire—nor of the occasions, so many were they, of Emily's death and the mournful vigil of her dog Keeper. (Tales of Emily's own violent savagery towards her dog came out only at the Black Bull when a 'friend of the family' had his tongue loosened by a drink, paid for, if reluctantly, by the firm of Thomas Cautley Newby.) It often seemed to the apprentice biographer that there was only a limited supply of stories about his subject—as there had been with Jesus: perhaps they could be told over and over again, and by different people, but they were actually the same—and sometimes Newby doubted whether Branwell, dead three months at the time of his first visit to the Parsonage, had not been a mythical son in the family.

All the assertions and repetitions of Branwell's genius led to a reverie—Newby could describe the odd sense of enlightenment which descended on him in that little room only in those terms, though he also admitted it had been the sight of the 'little lamp' trimmed so devotedly by Emily which inspired it. The lamp sat by the window (it had once been in the stone-flagged hall) and was known by now, in popular legend, to have been the guiding light for Branwell when he stumbled home from the inn. People spoke with reverence of the time passed by Emily as she waited for the return of her brother late at night; of three years expecting, as her poem declared, 'the messenger of Hope'. Newby had been shown the lines at the outset of his quest to write the life of Branwell . . . 'The little lamp burns straight, its rays shoot strong and far . . .'

The interview ends; Patrick Brontë falls silent and shuffles from the room. John Brown enquires, in cordial tone, whether Mr Newby will accompany him to the Black

Bull. It is clear that he has further 'proof' of Branwell
Brontë's authorship to divulge: his will be the most con-
troversial chapter in the biography. But Mr Newby refus-
es. He asks if he may visit Emily's room, the small study
above the downstairs room where once (though he does
not say so) he found the burning fragments of a book. Mr
Newby says he would like to look through some of the
Gondal poems, and understand the invented kingdom
inhabited by the youngest sister and Branwell. It will help
him to understand the genius of Branwell Brontë.

And John Brown, who says he is certain that the
Reverend Mr Brontë will have no objection at all, goes
down the winding stone stair and out across the hall of
the Parsonage into Church Lane.

EDITOR'S NOTE

We can come to no better conclusion as to the authorship of these fragments from the possible successor to Wuthering Heights *than did the suffering but resolute Henry Newby himself. Sometimes, it seems that Branwell Brontë is incontestably their creator; at others, a woman's hand is clearly indicated. Compassion for Henry, whose return visit to Haworth Parsonage was as gruelling as his first—if not more so, for he was 'hearing voices' by this stage—can be succeeded by relief that he found his vocation at last, passing from non-reader to one who devours novels and continuing through the fields of biography to discover his voice at last as a writer of historical fiction. In that mode, he may finally have discovered the truth of the impossible relationship between his hero, Heathcliff, and his heroine Emily Brontë.*

CHAPTER TWENTY

THE DEPOSITION OF HENRY NEWBY

I stayed a long time in the room where all those years ago I felt the presence of the just-dead Emily Brontë, and suffered—or so I thought—along with her at the cruel ending of a brilliant young life.

Now, I faced the cruel reality of another set of facts: the truth of the authorship of the novel published under the name of Ellis Bell—and, for that matter, the truth about the identity of those (or he or she) who had penned the chapters and pages I had found or had foisted upon me since my first coming to Haworth. And for this I suffered still more—so I regret to admit—than I had at learning of the early death of a young poet and writer: I suffered for my own character and the damage I permitted to be done in my name—viz. appending it to a volume of biography which set out to prove a lie. I knew —as well as the good John Brown and old Mr Brontë knew—that Branwell Brontë was not the author of *Wuthering Heights*; he might have invented some of the continuation of the story of those Godless people, for all I knew (and I did not wish to dwell on my youthful folly when it came to believing in their exploits and their passions), and he might yet supply a footnote in history as one who had followed his sister in her extraordinary venture. But Branwell was not a writer—he was more of a painter, I concluded, as I sat in that meagre study where genius had blossomed, and looked at his portrait of poor Emily. I could not and would not defame the true author of a masterpiece in order to please a publisher or for financial gain. Emily, with her 'little lamp' must shine unburnished for eternity.

Thoughts like these led me to sit on, while the day, a kind of spring day where the light is permanently on the edge of extinguishing itself altogether—the trees in the graveyard black still and sombre as spectral widows, a faint haze hanging around the path leading out to a darkened moor, and no sense of resolution to be seen anywhere—encouraged me to gaze longer at the portrait, this undecided also in its delineation of a young woman's earnest face. I knew, as I gazed, that I had seen this face; and I was aware, also, that this was an impossibility, for Emily had lain below me in the churchyard, as she did now, at the time of my first coming to the Parsonage. Yet —and as I contemplated her, she seemed to turn slightly and to direct a glance at me, as if surprised at some secret pleasure I might for an instant understand—I knew where I had seen her, and I shrank back into my chair.

The past—the winter of her death and of my walk in the snow to the shepherd's house, soaked but determined to find the truth of those characters I could not forget: this was where and how I had seen her. Up at the ruined farm of Top Withens—'Darkwall' Branwell termed the place, as if trying to convince listeners that he and he alone had brought the people and the setting to life— up in the fragments of a book that was an abandoned house, I had seen her kissing—and here I halted and rose to my feet. Already, the uncertain afternoon fled the garden of the Parsonage; there was no fire to get going in the grate; and I had no choice but to take her lamp to light me away from the house. For some power told me I was threatened, if I lingered even a minute longer, in the room.

Yet I did not go. I heard the voices, even as I began to cross the floor to the door; I heard them rise and then fall again, and I knelt by the end of the truckle bed to hear better through a crack in the planks there. I set down the lamp; and it seemed the voices flew up to me, like creatures of the night. I knelt, and looked down at a portion of the small study below.

'I did not die, and here's the proof of it!' The young woman who spoke was fair—fair as a Linton, I sensed in my heart already, but not calm as the family from The Grange had been known to be. She was wild—wilder than Cathy in the days of her long escapes to Peniston Crag, with the rain and the wind and young Heathcliff for company. 'You stole my son from my brother's house', Isabella went on—for it was she, it was she!—and I felt the thud of my heart against my ribs and then a long breathlessness. 'And I knew I would never have him back from a blackguard such as you, Heathcliff. Now you must return him to me. Today!'

How can I describe these people, in the brightly lit room that lay just seven or eight feet below me, but un-reachable, as if in deep transparent water, like a sunken ship. The passengers were ghosts—but they lived—and moved and spoke. And Isabella, in her dress as red as the fire which blazed behind her in the mirage of the little study, was more beautiful than ever she had been when in my dreams. Heathcliff—how could I have pitied the monster? how loved him also, wishing to extend a hand to this disfigured, corpulent reveller at a Black Sabbath of the soul—Heathcliff stood opposite my darling Isabella and laughed at her demands.

So Isabella told her secrets to the man who broke her heart, the man who stands in all weathers still at Gimmerton crossroads where the suicides are buried, and where he may meet his Cathy if the clouds are torn apart and a hag moon comes bobbing through. She told him of his mother—of Nelly's story—and of his father, Joseph Earnshaw; and he laughed even longer. 'What is it to me if I am?' he cried, and the flames leapt up to the mantel as if fanned from Hell. 'My Cathy—my little Cathy—is my daughter, and I begot her on my sister. She weds Linton tomorrow . . .'

'No!' Isabella's cry was piteous; in my attempt to struggle to my feet I overturned the little lamp and the light went out. I was now in complete blackness.

Linton, the son taken from Isabella, has Heathcliff as his father; and so, as Isabella knows, has young Catherine Linton. They should not marry; but they will.

I cannot say how much time passed before the scene beneath my feet melted away, a minute or maybe more. But for a time the voices rose with the March wind that whistled eerily outside on the moor and I heard the rage and grief of Isabella and the laughter of the fiend who had brought a curse to her family, the Lintons, and to the Earnshaws up at Top Withens.

EDITOR'S NOTE

After his death from consumption in 1861, Henry Newby was seen to have left a chapter of either biography or fiction (it is hard to tell which) entitled The Rape of Gondal. *We present it here for the interest of future scholars.*

CHAPTER TWENTY-ONE

THE RAPE OF GONDAL
by Henry Newby

The bedroom corridor at Haworth smells of fat; beef dripping stored in a jar in the larder by Tabby and scooped out for frying up the potatoes the Reverend Patrick likes to eat for supper on Saturdays. The smell comes down from the pulpit on Sunday morning, when hellfire is threatened for sins too terrible to bear telling of again, these long known about by all the parish: the robbery up at The Heights where one of the thieves, face blackened, plunged a knife into the chest of Jonas Pickles; the birth of a baby to the Heaton family who had to pay the defecting father to marry the girl; incest down at Rush Isles where another Heaton, Betty, had married her stepbrother John Shackleton. The strong, stale smell comes from the mouth of God and is a slow and painful punishment for the dreams and fantasies and crimes committed by those who try to fight free from the limits and constrictions of a righteous life. Now, as Emily lies awake in the bed she had until a few days ago shared with her elder sister Charlotte, the smell creeps along the bedroom passage and slides under the door. Saturday night prepares for Sunday morning. On the ground floor of the house, where her father's study contains the hunched figure and wild disorder of papers of his Sabbath sermon, Patrick Brontë sits wrapped in the comforting, familiar

smell. It reminds him of his dead wife, Mary. Her sister
Aunt Branwell was a Cornishwoman, who had liked to
make pasties in the cramped kitchen. She had tried to
persuade Tabby to do the same. But Tabby is faithful to
the wishes of her Irish-born employer. At Haworth, the
Reverend Patrick will never lack potatoes: pasties don't
go down well with him at all. Potatoes, eaten boiled for
the midday meal, will continue for eternity to be fried on
Saturday nights in dripping.

Emily, at twelve, is the second youngest of the six
Brontë children. Tonight, the 20th of January, is also her
second night alone. For Charlotte, two years her senior,
has now gone off to school at Roe Head; and their shared
bed, so lately a theatre, a magic cave filled with stories
and adventures, is empty and cold. There is nothing left
in the house to concentrate on but the smell—deathly
now, to Emily's imagination: an omen of the dreariness
and desolation of the coming year. January, with its two-
faced god, leers at her from the dark window where the
rosy curtains Aunt Branwell made after Maria and Elizabeth died fail to meet in the middle, and so let in spectres
and bogeys, all the roaming spirits of the moors. The
smell turns to a white vapour, a creeping shroud, and
envelops Emily as she lies in blankets and sheets so
rough with starch her legs are rubbed raw with her
attempts to run away and escape in her sleep. Is there a
sound, a movement, on the landing outside her room? It
is even blacker out there than in the garden, high above
Withens, where the ghost of the miserable Heaton girl,
dead since giving birth to her unwanted baby, walks and
weeps at night with her poor mother. Is the handle of the
bedroom door, fastened a hundred times a day by Tabby
when it slips from the lock (there is no man in the household to perform these menial tasks: Branwell, the only
boy, is as excitable and Irish as the rest of Patrick's fam-

ily, and the clergyman himself too preoccupied with sin and redemption to attend to a faulty door handle)—is the door about to swing open, as it terrifyingly does, even on a windless night, revealing the horror of black nothingness, the void? Charlotte has always been there, when it does. But now, Emily, wide awake and lying flat beneath the sheets, is alone. She feels the clammy persistence of the smell, as it coils across her legs and lays itself on the quilt. She screams—but, as in all the most terrifying tales concocted by her elder siblings, Branwell and Charlotte—no sound comes.

The bedroom door opens, and then closes again. The smell grows stronger before receding, its tail slithering over the bed and landing with a thump on the bare boards before vanishing altogether. Another presence replaces it: a presence as well known to Emily as the odour of potatoes-and-dripping that has come to stand for all she dreads, hates—and once, when her mother Mary was alive, had loved. But, as it comes towards her and fastens on her face, she does this time scream aloud. The presence has cold lips; and they land on her own like stone. Tabby, far away in the kitchen, can of course hear nothing. If the Reverend Patrick hears a sound, he does nothing about it. Aren't the children always shrieking and play-acting, in the world he knows, somehow, they must learn to leave if they are to grow up to be responsible adults? Emily's scream, to Patrick, is another melodramatic expression from the kingdom he has heard referred to as Angria. He resolves to stamp it out—but at present he has his sermon to write, and besides, as he will never admit to Aunt Branwell, he is suffering from indigestion, from eating too many of those richly fried potatoes, glistening in their bed of fat.

Alexander Percy, Earl of Northangerland, is six feet
tall with auburn hair, a fine aquiline nose and the air of
command to be expected from one who conquers wherever he goes—whether in Nigrittia, province of the Afri-
can realm so densely populated with earls, dukes, Border
chieftains and lovely, languishing maidens—or in the
country of James Hogg and Walter Scott, the mountain-
ous areas where the Brontë children place their imaginations. No one—and nothing—can overpower Alexander
Percy, once Alexander Rogue and before that, in an early
incarnation, Alexander Naughty. He is the son of the
Border Ballad, the scion of *Blackwood's Magazine* where
the most violent and ghoulish stories of those great
writers and tale-tellers, appear regularly, to be pounced on
and read again and again. Alexander Percy, with his
habitual sneer and his passionate nature when aroused,
is the terror of the neighbourhood, the lord and master of
all he surveys.

The dark valley of the Yarrow, the wide river that
flows down from the ghost-filled hills of the Ettrick shepherd, James Hogg, poet and author of *The Memoirs of A
Justified Sinner*, lies before Percy, Earl of Northangerland
as he strides towards his next conquest. For long now,
the hero with flaming hair has courted the Lady Augusta
Segovia, and now the time has come to seize her, pillage
the sweet modesty of which Emily and Branwell, col-
laborating in the long odes and ballads dedicated to Lady
Augusta, have made much; and then watch her die, to be
succeeded in Lord Percy's affections by her cousin
Harriet. There comes a question of rivals fighting for the
hand of Augusta—but Percy neither cares nor remem-
bers how the last, breathless confabulation might have
gone.

For the Earl of Northangerland, the diminutive, be-
spectacled Branwell Brontë, has at thirteen years of age
discovered the truth of the 'bad things' for which the

great Lord Byron had been known. Neither John Brown, the handsome sexton's son at Haworth, nor Aunt Branwell, who professes herself, being a Cornishwoman, more attuned to the ways of the world than her brother-in-law —have done other than turn away and change the subject when the name of Lord Byron comes up. But Branwell, now transmogrifying from Alexander Percy to the great poet himself, has found and ordered the volume which outlines his hero's crimes.

It is past midnight when the Earl leaves the valley of the Black Douglas's castle, crosses the Yarrow on his foaming steed, and arrives on the shores of St Mary's Loch. He dismounts and looks about him, as is customary before a raid; and it is as George Gordon, Lord Byron, that he swaggers down the bedroom passage and tries the faulty handle on Lady Augusta's door. . . .

THE END